What is a trolley car family? A family that lives in a trolley car, of course!

That's what the Parkers decide to do—Ma and Pa Parker and Bill, George, Sally and Peter Parker too.

Pa Parker drives a trolley car.

Trolley cars used to go clanging down streets of most American towns and cities. Then cars and buses took their place. But Pa Parker loves his trolley car. He won't give it up to drive a bus. So off go the Parkers in their trolley car home. It's just for a little while, they say. If only they knew the surprises that lie ahead.

THE TROLLEY CAR FAMILY

Eleanor Clymer

Illustrated by Ursula Koering

AN
APPLE
PAPERBACK

SCHOLASTIC INC.
New York Toronto London Auckland Sydney

ISBN 0-590-40732-5

12 11 10 9 8 7   3 4 5 6 7/9

Printed in the U.S.A.   40

CONTENTS

1. THE NOISY PARKERS

MR. JEFFERSON was a cross man. He was cross in the morning, and he was cross at night. He was cross when he met people, and he was cross when he was alone, which was most of the time.

Mr. Jefferson was a milkman in the little town of East Sawyerville. He had to get up in the dark, and go out and hitch up his horse, while everybody else was sound asleep in bed. Then he had to drive to the dairy and get his milk. Then he had to drive around delivering the milk.

At four o'clock in the morning, his bony white horse could be heard clop-clopping through the quiet streets of East Sawyerville. Mr. Jefferson would walk along the sidewalk from one door to the next, by the light of the street lamps, leaving bottles of milk and cream.

When he was all finished, he would climb up on the seat of the milk wagon, pull his old hat down over his eyes, and slap the reins on the horse's back. The horse would start for home.

People would be getting up now. They would come out and take in their milk, and call "Good Morning" to Mr. Jefferson as he went by. Mr. Jefferson would grunt in reply and slap the reins on the horse's back again.

"Got to get home and get some sleep," he would mutter to the horse. "Can't stay out here all day talking."

The horse would amble along. And just as he was turning in at the driveway that led to the stable behind the house, out would come the Parkers!

It was the Parkers who made Mr. Jefferson cross, though they certainly didn't know it, and would have been very much surprised if anybody had told them. The reason was that there were such a lot of them, and they made so much noise.

They lived in a little house next door to Mr. Jefferson. Their house was much too small for them, but they didn't mind. They were always jolly and noisy, especially the first thing in the morning, just when Mr. Jefferson was feeling sleepiest and crossest.

Mr. Parker was a motorman for the trolley car company. And that was why they liked their little house, even though it *was* too small for them. For it was only two blocks from the car barn, and the trolley tracks went right past the door.

Every morning, just as Mr. Jefferson was coming home, the door of the Parkers' house would open and all of them would come bouncing out on the porch.

Then a trolley car would come along. Clang! the bell

All of them would come bouncing out on the porch.

would go. There would be Pa at the wheel. He would wave to his family, and they would all wave back and shout, "Good-by, Pa!"

Then the car would rattle away and the Parkers would go back inside. But that didn't mean they would be quiet. Oh, no!

First there would be the rattle of dishes being washed. Then they would shout to each other up and down the stairs. Then some of them would come out to play, and they would yell to the others who stayed inside.

And meanwhile, in his house next door, Mr. Jefferson would be muttering to himself over his lonesome breakfast, "I know I won't be able to sleep with that racket going on."

On weekdays, of course, the older children went to school. But then, just as Mr. Jefferson managed to doze off, about lunch time, back they would come, laughing and calling out to each other.

Saturdays and Sundays were the worst. Then the children were all at home, and Mr. Jefferson found it hard to get a wink of sleep.

There were six in the family. First, of course, there was Mr. Parker. He wore a motorman's cap and a big mustache. Then there was Mrs. Parker. She was short and plump, and usually wore a checkered apron. Red and white checks were her favorite, though she sometimes wore other colors. She was so busy that she didn't often have time to take her apron off.

Sally, the oldest child, had short yellow braids and brown eyes. She was eleven.

Bill was ten. He was a big boy for his age, with broad shoulders and strong arms and legs. He was proud of his muscles and planned to be a baseball player when he grew up.

George, who was eight, was just the opposite of Bill. He was thin, with straight yellow hair and a far-away look in his eyes. He didn't always answer when he was spoken to, because he was often so busy with his own ideas that he didn't hear.

Peter, the baby, was two.

The children all said "Hello" to Mr. Jefferson whenever they met him. But he usually just grunted in reply. He didn't want to encourage them.

Sometimes on Sundays the whole Parker family would turn out for a picnic. Then Mr. Jefferson would say to himself, "Ah, now I have a chance to get a nap."

All six Parkers would pour out of their little house, each one carrying something. Picnic baskets, baseball bats, umbrellas, kites. They would stand on the porch till a trolley car came along, and then they would all climb on board and go for a ride. Mr. Jefferson couldn't see why Mr. Parker, who drove a trolley car every day, should want to go for a trolley car ride on his day off. He would wait till they were all out, and then settle down for his nap.

But for some reason, he couldn't sleep when they were gone either. Maybe it was too quiet. Maybe he

missed the good smell of cake baking that so often came from Mrs. Parker's kitchen. Anyway, he would find himself waiting till they got home in the evening, all tired out, with dirty faces and empty picnic baskets, and little Peter sound asleep on his father's shoulder.

Next morning, everything would be back to normal. Mr. Jefferson would be crossly muttering about the noisy neighbors, and the Parkers would be loudly calling "Good morning" to him and wondering what made him so cross.

"Mama," Sally would report, "I said hello to Mr. Jefferson when I took in the milk, and he just said, 'Um.'"

"Poor man," her mother would say, shaking her head, "he's got nobody to cook him a good hot breakfast. Living all alone like that! Goodness knows when he gets a good meal."

"Couldn't I take him some biscuits?" Sally would ask.

"Of course," said Mrs. Parker. "But don't disturb him."

"Leave the plate on the porch and run back," George advised.

But Sally would not do that. She always knocked at the door and waited till Mr. Jefferson opened it a crack and peered out.

"Some biscuits my mother just made," she would say.

Mr. Jefferson would mumble, "Thanks," and take the plate and shut the door as soon as possible.

"I think he just *wants* to be cross," Sally said to her family.

Mr. Parker thought it was because he worked at night and slept in the daytime.

"It's not natural for a man," he said.

But Ma said no. "It's just that he's got so used to living alone and being lonesome," she said. "He's afraid if he gets used to company, he'll want it all the time."

"Well, what's wrong with that?" Bill asked.

"Nothing wrong," said Ma. "But it's not for us to tell him what's good for him and what isn't. So you children just leave him alone until such time as he decides to be sociable."

But all forbidden things are bound to be interesting, and the more you try to walk away from them, the more likely they are to pop right up in front of you.

For instance, there was Mr. Jefferson's horse, Whitey. Bill was very much interested in the horse, who, when he wasn't working, liked to stand with his head sticking out of a window in the stable. Then he could look around and see what was going on. He was a friendly horse.

Bill and George liked to stand on the other side of the fence and talk to the horse. The horse would wag his head up and down, or blow through his lips at them.

"I'd like to go over and pat him," said Bill one day, "even if I can't ride him."

"Guess Mr. Jefferson wouldn't like that," said George.

The two were leaning over the fence eating apples.

"Let's give him a piece of apple," said George.

"How you going to do that without going over there?" Bill asked.

George looked around. His eye fell on his little brother Peter digging in a corner of the yard. He borrowed Peter's shovel. He put the apple on the shovel and held it out to Whitey. The handle was just long enough to reach. Whitey got the apple between his big lips and munched it. He wagged his head up and down and whinnied.

"He wants more," said Bill. He grabbed the shovel, placed his apple in it, and held it out. But he was in too much of a hurry. He dropped the apple. Then he reached for it and dropped the shovel.

Little Peter saw his shovel on the other side of the fence and began to scream. "My shovel!" he yelled.

"Wait, Peter," said Bill.

"My shovel," Peter bellowed.

Whitey stamped in his stall and whinnied again.

Bill climbed over the fence to get the shovel. Sally looked out of the window and called, "Bill, you come back here! You're not allowed to do that!"

"My shovel!" Peter wept.

"Keep quiet, all of you!" Bill shouted. "You'll wake up Mr. Jefferson."

Just then Mr. Jefferson's bedroom window banged open, and Mr. Jefferson's face appeared, very cross.

"What's the matter down there?" he growled at them. "Can't a man ever get any sleep?"

Old Whitey looked up at his master in the window. He whinnied, *"Heh-heh-heh-heh!"* It sounded exactly as if he were laughing. Mr. Jefferson banged the window down.

Bill gave the apple to Whitey and climbed back into his own yard. His mother was standing on the back steps.

"It's too bad," she said, "that that poor man had to go and live right next to a family of children like you. But it can't be helped, and I don't want any of you going over there. And that's final."

"But the horse—" Bill began.

"Maybe some time when you're bigger," said his mother, "you can go to a farm and get real friendly with some horses. But in the meantime you'll have to be content with just looking at the horse."

Then there was the time the Parkers' cat had kittens.

"Can't a man ever get any sleep?" Mr. Jefferson growled.

There were three of them, coal black, like their mother. Little Peter loved the kittens so much that he almost choked them with his hugs. As soon as the kittens could run, they learned to run away when they saw him coming. And of course the family did all they could to teach Peter that he had to be careful. But Peter could run faster than the kittens, and he loved them so much that the sight of them chased all other ideas out of his curly little head.

One day the kittens disappeared. The children looked everywhere for them, but they simply weren't to be found. The house was searched from cellar to attic. So was the yard, and the woodshed. The mother cat appeared at lunch time, ate her lunch and went to sleep. The children watched her in order to follow her when she woke up and went back to her babies. But she was too smart for them. She disappeared too, when they forgot to watch her for a minute.

"Kitty, kitty, kitty!" Peter called, sadly, walking around and around the yard, and looking under every stick and stone.

"I bet I know where they are," said George. "I bet she took them over to Mr. Jefferson's house. She knows we can't go over there."

"Maybe they're in the stable," said Bill. "You go over and look. But don't make any noise."

George didn't climb over the fence. He crept cautiously around the end, and then edged toward the stable, keeping close to the fence on Mr. Jefferson's side. He got safely inside the stable without being noticed. Whitey stamped his feet a bit but he didn't whinny.

It was fairly dark inside the stable. George stepped quietly around, but he could see no sign of any cats. He peered into all the dark corners. But of course the cats were black, and couldn't be easily seen without a light. Why hadn't he brought a flashlight?

George climbed up a short ladder that led to the little hayloft. He felt about in the hay. Suddenly he saw something glowing, like a little light. Then he saw

. . . . making the most awful noise!

some more little lights, green and round. Why, they were the cats' eyes glowing in the dark.

"*Miaow!*" said three little voices.

He stuffed all three kittens inside his shirt and climbed down the ladder. But the kittens clawed at him and tickled his ribs, inside his shirt, and he giggled and missed the lowest rung, and fell, knocking over a couple of feed buckets and making the most awful noise.

Whitey stamped and whinnied, the kittens squealed,

and Bill, waiting on the other side of the fence, called out, "Are you all right, Georgie?"

George came out, face to face with Mr. Jefferson, who had come down to see who was breaking into his stable.

"The kittens ran away," George explained.

"I don't blame them," said Mr. Jefferson, crossly. "They probably wanted a little peace and quiet." And he turned and walked back into his house.

The children didn't think that was quite fair.

"If he hadn't been so cross," said George, "I could have asked him to let me look in his stable, and then I wouldn't have had to be so quiet. It's always when you're trying too hard to be quiet that you make the biggest noise."

2. MR. JEFFERSON PAYS A VISIT

SO THINGS went on from day to day. The mother cat finally took her babies to live somewhere else, and Pa brought home a stuffed cat that Peter could hug as much as he liked. And Mr. Jefferson had just about gotten used to the idea that the Parkers would always be noisy, and he would just have to keep on being cross about it.

But one morning, when Mr. Jefferson was driving home, grumpy as usual, he was surprised to find that their house was really very quiet. No cheerful voices shouted back and forth. No doors slammed.

Mr. Jefferson drove his horse into the stable and unhitched. He pulled down some hay and measured some oats into the feed box. Then he went back to his house and put some coffee on to boil.

It was time for the trolley car to come along. But nobody ran out on the porch, and no wheels rattled on the track.

"It doesn't seem right," Mr. Jefferson kept saying to himself. "No, it just doesn't seem right at all."

And then suddenly he said, "Maybe something is wrong!"

He went out on his porch and looked over toward the Parkers' house. Then he went down the steps and across the yard. Then he stopped. Then he went up the steps and rang the Parkers' bell.

Sally came to the door. "Why, hello, Mr. Jefferson," she said.

"Hello," said Mr. Jefferson. "Is anything the matter?"

"I don't know," said Sally. She looked puzzled.

"Didn't see anybody out this morning," said Mr. Jefferson, gruffly. "Wondered if anybody was sick."

"No," said Sally. "Nobody's sick. Only Pa didn't go to work this morning, and he's still sitting at the table and drinking coffee, and Ma can't get the dishes washed, and she says she doesn't know what we're going to do."

"Going to do about what?" Mr. Jefferson asked.

"I don't know," said Sally.

"Well," said Mr. Jefferson, "I was just wondering." And he turned to go home again.

But just then Mrs. Parker's voice called from the kitchen. "Who's there, Sally?"

"It's Mr. Jefferson, Ma," said Sally. "He wanted to know if anything was the matter with us."

"Well, bring him in here," said Mrs. Parker. "Don't keep him standing there, child."

"Come on in," said Sally, smiling at Mr. Jefferson. "Right this way." There was nothing for him to do, then, but to follow her to the kitchen.

"How do, Mr. Jefferson," said Mrs. Parker, smiling at him too, but looking a little worried at the same time.

Mr. Parker sat at the round table in the middle of the room, stirring a cup of coffee. He didn't look at all cheerful. Bill and George sat on a bench by the window. Little Peter sat under the table playing with some tin cans. Every few minutes he would bang one against the other.

"How do," said Mr. Parker, gloomily.

"Won't you sit down, Mr. Jefferson?" Mrs. Parker asked.

Mr. Jefferson scowled. "Oh, no, thanks," he muttered. "Have to be getting back. Just stopped in to see if everything was all right. I mean, you know—"

Mrs. Parker laughed. "I know what you mean. It's too quiet over here."

"Well, yes," said Mr. Jefferson. "But if you're all right, I'll be getting back. Have to get my breakfast, you know, and get some sleep."

"I've just made some fresh coffee," said Mrs. Parker, "and I'd be pleased if you'd have some, with a piece of cake."

Mr. Jefferson sat down. There was nothing else he could do. Mrs. Parker poured some coffee for him. Then she went into the pantry and came back with a plate of cake.

"Have some cake," she said. "I always think there's nothing like cake to cheer you up. Come on, Pa, have some cake."

Mr. Parker took a slice, and so did Mr. Jefferson.

"What kind is that, Ma?" Bill asked.

"It's marble cake," said his mother. She passed the plate to each of the children.

"Can you play marbles with it?" George asked.

Bill and Sally giggled.

"This is no time for nonsense," their mother observed. "If you can't behave, you can go outdoors."

Mr. Jefferson took a sip of his coffee. It was very good. Much better than the kind he made himself.

"Aren't they going to school?" he asked.

"I thought they'd better stay home," said Mrs. Parker. "We are going to have a family conference, and I thought they should take part. You never can tell; children often have good ideas."

"Ideas!" said Mr. Jefferson.

"I know what you're thinking," said Mrs. Parker. "You think they have too many ideas as it is. Well, that's just because they're young and have to learn how to think. But some of their ideas are very sensible."

Mr. Jefferson just said, "Hm!"

Mr. Parker and Mrs. Parker looked at each other for a moment in a worried manner, and then Mr. Parker said, "Well, Mary, go ahead and tell him. It won't do any harm."

The children stopped chewing their cake and lis-

"We're going to have a family conference," Pa said.

tened quietly. Only little Peter banged his cans together under the table. Mr. Jefferson winced.

"Don't mind him," said Mrs. Parker. "It'll be quiet
enough around here pretty soon. You see, we may
have to move."

"Move!" said Mr. Jefferson. "What for?"

"Well, it's like this," said Mrs. Parker. "John here is
a motorman for the street car company."

"I know that," said Mr. Jefferson.

"Perhaps you have heard," Mrs. Parker went on,

"that they are going to take away the street cars and put in busses."

"Did read about it in the paper," said Mr. Jefferson. "What will happen to Mr. Parker?"

"Mm!" said Mr. Parker, with his mouth full of cake. "That's the question."

"If he could drive a bus," said Mrs. Parker, "he could keep his job, but he won't drive a bus."

"Why not?" Mr. Jefferson asked.

"Always hated the durned things," said Mr. Parker. "They won't stay on a track. You never know what they'll do, careening all over the street. Now with a street car, you know where you are. All other traffic has to get out of the way. But with these busses, the cars are all the time swooping in and out around you. I don't like it."

"I really can't say I blame him," said Mrs. Parker. "I never did like to see a man do something he didn't like."

"Well, where are you going to move?" Mr. Jefferson asked.

Mrs. Parker looked at Mr. Parker.

"Go on, speak up, Mary," said Mr. Parker.

"Well, it's like this," said Mrs. Parker. "John's been with the company a long time."

"Twenty years," said Mr. Parker.

"So they said he could have a month's pay."

"That wouldn't last long with this big family," said Mr. Jefferson.

Mrs. Parker laughed. "It won't last at all," she said. "He didn't take it. What do you think he took?"

"What did you take, Pa?" said George, Bill and Sally, for they couldn't keep still any longer.

"Tell them, Mary," said Mr. Parker.

"He asked them for his old street car," said Mrs. Parker.

The children stared at him with open mouths and popping eyes. Then they burst out, "You did! Boy, that was a wonderful idea! Did they give it to you?"

"Be quiet, children," said their mother. "Yes, they said he could have it. He loves that street car like one of his own children. Only we don't know just what to do with it, and that's why we don't know where we're going to move, or anything."

"It does seem like a hard thing to decide," said Mr. Jefferson.

"That's why we need all the ideas we can get," said Mrs. Parker. "You can't drive around in it, and it's too big to put in the back yard. Why, it's a lot bigger than this house."

"Don't like to sell it either," said Mr. Parker.

"I don't know who would buy it," said his wife.

"Couldn't we live in it?" Sally asked.

Everybody looked at her.

"Sure, why not?" said Bill.

Ma looked as if somebody had handed her a hot pan and she didn't know whether to put it down or drop it.

"We'd save rent," she said at last. "If we could only find a place to put it."

"If it was out in the country," said Bill, "we'd have room for a baseball diamond."

"We could go swimming," said George.

"That's right," said his mother. "If there was a place to swim. That would save heating bath water. In summer, that is."

"Of course, summer is all it would be good for," said Mr. Parker. "Just while I was looking for a new job."

"And I'm sure you'll find one," said Mrs. Parker, comfortingly. "But where would be the best place for the trolley?"

They all sat and thought. Then Sally said, "I know! The picnic place!"

Everybody stared at her. Then they all exclaimed, "Why, of course! The picnic place! Or some place out there!"

Mr. Jefferson looked puzzled. "What's that?" he asked.

Ma explained. "When we go on picnics on Sunday," she said, "we ride to the end of the car line. Out beyond the other side of town, you know. Then we get off. There's an old track that goes on to the next town, Taylorville."

"Used to be an interurban," said Pa, taking another piece of cake. He was beginning to look a little more cheerful.

"They never use it any more," said Ma. "It's all

rusty. The track, I mean. The street car company bought up a lot of land out that way. I don't know what they were going to do with it. Build car barns out in the country where the taxes would be cheap, I guess. Now if we could rent a bit of land and if we could tow the car out there—"

Mr. Parker sighed. "No power out that way any more," he said. "Just an old dirt road the farmers use. And we couldn't tow it with a truck."

"Why not, Pa?" Bill asked.

"Car has to go on rails," said Pa, "and the rails would ruin the truck tires."

All the Parkers looked downcast. How could they get the car out into the country if there wasn't any power? The baby Peter stuck his head out from under the table. He couldn't understand what was going on. One minute the family would be shouting, and the next minute they would all get quiet and sad. Peter looked from one to the other. Then he looked at Mr. Jefferson. He knew Mr. Jefferson was the man who drove the milk wagon.

"Horse!" he said, putting his hand on Mr. Jefferson's knee.

"Of course!" said Mr. Jefferson. "That's the answer."

"*What's* the answer?" Mr. Parker asked. He hadn't been paying attention to Peter.

"Horses," said Mr. Jefferson. "I've got a horse, and if you can get another one somewhere, that's all the power you'll need."

"Hooray!" Bill shouted.

"All we need is another horse!" said George.

Sally got down on the floor and put her arms around Peter. "It was all your idea," she said. "You deserve another piece of cake."

"Cake!" cried Peter.

"Now wait a minute, children," said Mrs. Parker. "Do you mean you'll lend us your horse, Mr. Jefferson?"

Mr. Jefferson was just putting a piece of cake into his mouth. He stopped suddenly and stared at Mrs. Parker. He'd gone and offered them the use of his horse!

There was no way of getting out of it now. "Well, yes," he said, scratching his chin.

"Well, it's an ill wind that blows no good," said Ma. "If we move, it'll be nice and quiet around here."

Mr. Jefferson tried to pretend he hadn't heard this, but George piped up. "But, Ma, suppose some other family with a lot of children moves in here, what will Mr. Jefferson do then?"

"Keep still, George," said his mother. "You talk too much."

"Where could we get another horse?" Bill asked. "Pa, do you know anybody that has a horse?"

Mr. Parker shook his head. "I'll try to find out," he said. "Maybe some of the men down at the car barn know where to hire a horse." He sighed. "When I was a boy your age, Bill, we had three horses on our farm. They don't use horses much any more. Only for riding or for milk wagons."

Mr. Jefferson got up quickly and walked to the door. Then he said, "Maybe I can find another horse. Got to be going now. Thanks for the cake. Got to get some sleep." And he opened the door and went out, as if he were afraid he might change his mind.

When he had gone, the Parker family sat and looked at each other. There was surprise in their faces, but for a few seconds they said nothing. Then they all began to talk at once.

"Well, what do you think of that?"

"He wasn't cross at all!"

"And he'll lend us his horse!"

"Oh, boy! Will we have fun!"

Then Ma said, "I'll be sorry to leave this place, we've been here so long. But it's an ill wind that blows no good, as I said before. Here we've been living next door to Mr. Jefferson all this time, and it wasn't until we were in trouble that he came to the door to see what he could do to help."

"That's right," said Sally. "He didn't *have* to come and ring the bell when we weren't making any noise. But of course once he had rung it he couldn't help coming in."

"He could have thought of some excuse if he'd wanted to," said Ma. "Now you kids let him alone and don't pester him too much, and he'll turn out to be real sociable yet. Mark my words. I don't think that man has a cross disposition at all. He's just so softhearted he's ashamed to show it, for he's afraid he won't be able to say no."

She began clearing the table. Then she looked at the clock. "It's only ten minutes to nine," she remarked, "so you children may as well go to school."

"Oh, Ma, you said we shouldn't," Bill complained.

Ma wasted no time in argument. "Go along now, and don't be any later than you can help. I thought the conference would last all morning, but it hasn't, so you may as well go and get your education."

3. THE PLANS ARE LAID

SALLY, BILL and George could hardly wait for school to be over that day. At least three times during the morning and four times during the afternoon, each of them had to be told by the teacher to stop wriggling and pay attention. And when the three o'clock bell finally did ring, all three of them ran so fast that they almost bumped into each other at the gate. They ran all the way home. There was Ma sitting on the front porch, calmly rocking, with Peter in her lap.

"My goodness, Ma, how can you sit there like that?" Sally demanded. "Where's Pa?"

"He went to the street car company."

"You mean to find out about the land?" said Bill.

"Yes."

"And he hasn't come home yet?"

"No."

"Did he find another horse?"

"I don't know."

"There he comes now," said George.

The three children raced up the street to meet him. Pa looked much more cheerful than he had looked that morning. In fact, he was grinning. He wouldn't say a word until he had climbed the porch steps and sat down in the other rocking chair.

"Well, Pa?" Sally asked.

"Well, what?" said Pa, in a very aggravating tone.

"Well, what did they say?"

"They said all right," said Pa. "They said they'd rent us some land. For the whole summer." Then he stopped.

The children waited for him to go on. They sat down on the steps.

"Well, tell us the whole story," said Ma, impatiently. "Whenever you have something real interesting to tell, you keep stopping and starting, just like your own street car."

"All right," said Pa. "They said that there's an old farm about ten miles from the edge of town, between here and Taylorville. That's farther'n we ever walked for a picnic, away out from the end of this car line. Farm belongs to the car company. They were going to have a car barn there but they never did. Just let it lay. Say they'll rent it to us."

"Is there a house there?" Ma asked.

"No." Pa shook his head. "House burned down or fell apart or something. Just the land and some kind of shed or barn."

"When can we go?" Bill asked. He didn't care about houses. All he wanted was a baseball diamond.

"Is there a place to swim?" George asked.

Peter climbed up on his father's knee. "Horse?" he inquired.

Sally laughed. "He thinks every time he says 'horse' we'll all take notice of him."

"That's true," said Pa. "All we need now is a couple of horses. I couldn't find anybody that knew about horses."

"Horse!" said Peter. "Horse over dere!" He pointed over to Mr. Jefferson's yard.

The family looked. There was Mr. Jefferson himself on the other side of the fence.

Sally laughed and hugged Peter. "That's Mr. Jefferson, honey. Hello, Mr. Jefferson! We can have the land! Pa just found out!"

"But we haven't got a horse yet," said Bill.

"Well, I was over to the dairy company this morning," said Mr. Jefferson.

"That's when you're supposed to sleep," George interrupted.

"Hush, Georgie," said Ma. "Don't interrupt."

"Well, I couldn't get to sleep," said Mr. Jefferson. "So I went over there, and it seems they have a couple of extra horses that aren't working this week, and they'll lend us one."

Pa said, "That was real nice of you, Mr. Jefferson. I

could have gone over there myself. But I'm much obliged to you."

"That's all right," said Mr. Jefferson. "I figured they knew me, and if they had a horse they'd let me have him. I'm the only milkman that has his own horse, and that saves them a lot of money, seeing they don't have to feed him, so they don't mind lending me a horse."

"Well, if you lend us your Whitey, and we get this other horse from the dairy, we're all set," said Pa. "Soon as I get the car towed out to where we're going, I'll get the horses back to you."

"How are you going to do that, Pa?" George asked.

"Why, I'll ride one and lead the other," said Pa. "Think I can't ride a horse?"

"No, Pa, but how will you get back to the car?"

"Why, I'll ride my bicycle. I'll leave the bicycle here, and then ride it back."

"That's a very smart idea," said Ma.

But Sally said, "I have a better one. Why doesn't Mr. Jefferson come with us?"

Everybody stared at her. Then Bill burst out, "That's a swell idea!" And Pa and Ma nodded and said, "It certainly is. What about it, Mr. Jefferson?"

Mr. Jefferson looked puzzled, just as he had that morning when he found himself offering the Parkers his horse.

"Oh, now, I don't know," he said, scowling. "Now wait a minute. I don't think I could do that—"

"Oh, why not?" Sally cried. She ran down the steps and over to the fence. "We'd have a lot of fun. And I bet you need a vacation. And we'd be very quiet. We'd let you sleep as much as you wanted."

"Hm!" said Mr. Jefferson. He was trying to look very cross. But he wasn't succeeding very well. "Well, all right!" he muttered. "Guess I do need a vacation. I'll do it. But only for a few days. Can't spare more time than that."

"Now, Mr. Jefferson," said Ma, "you ought to take at least a week. You haven't had a change in a long time. You've been working at night and sleeping in the daytime—"

"Trying to sleep, you mean," said Pa.

"You ought to get some sunshine on you," Ma went on, "and a good hot breakfast in the morning."

"Maybe you're right," said Mr. Jefferson. "Maybe I do need a rest. I'll think about it. Then Whitey could have a vacation too, after he got done hauling the trolley car."

"Hooray!" shouted Bill. Now he would have Whitey around for a whole week.

That evening, after supper, Bill and George were having batting practice out in the yard. Ma and Pa were sitting on the porch. Sally was playing ball with Peter to keep him out of the boys' way.

Suddenly Bill stopped, with his bat in the air, and called, "Look at Mr. Jefferson!"

. . . . then Whitey could have a vacation, too.

There was Mr. Jefferson leaning on the fence. He had a big straw hat stuck on the back of his head.

"Hello," Mr. Jefferson called back. And then, as they watched, something happened. Something that had not happened in a long time. His face wrinkled up and his mouth stretched, and he grinned at them. It wasn't much of a grin, but it *was* a grin!

Then he spoke. "It's all settled. I'm taking a week's vacation. I'm not used to being up all day and in bed all night, and I might not like it. But I'm willing to try."

The children all shouted, "Hooray! Oh, boy!"

At the noise, old Whitey stuck his long white face out of the window of his stable, and then they all laughed so hard that the tears ran down their cheeks. Whitey had a little straw hat on, just like Mr. Jefferson's. Only Whitey's hat had two holes in the brim for his ears to stick through.

"What's that for?" Sally asked, as soon as she could talk.

"If you'll stop laughing," said Mr. Jefferson, "I'll explain. Whitey is a night horse. He's not used to the sun. I don't want him to get sunstroke. And if he's going to pull a big old trolley car out in the middle of a field somewhere, he's got to wear his sun hat."

Whitey tossed his head and whinnied: *Heh-heh-heh-heh!*

"Sounds as if he's laughing too," said Bill.

"It sounds that way," said Mr. Jefferson, "but he isn't. I can tell when he's laughing."

"What's he doing, then?" Bill asked.

"He's complaining," said Mr. Jefferson. "He doesn't like the hat."

"Oh, let's give him something to make him feel better," said Sally. "I'll get some sugar."

"I have some right here," said Mr. Jefferson, putting his hand in his pocket. "Always carry it with me."

Bill climbed over the fence and took the lump of sugar

from Mr. Jefferson. He held it out to Whitey, whose big soft lips tickled the palm of his hand. Bill stroked the long smooth nose.

"I never thought," said George, "that Bill would be on that side of the fence with Mr. Jefferson standing there and watching him."

Everybody laughed at that, except Mrs. Parker. She got up from her chair and walked to the end of the porch.

"Georgie," she said, "we all know what you meant by what you said just now, only you didn't say it quite right. That's why we laughed. But I want to tell Mr. Jefferson the same thing, only in a different way.

"Mr. Jefferson," she went on, "we've been neighbors for a long time, and somehow we never got to be friendly. But it seems people have to be in trouble before they learn to know their real friends, and you have certainly proved to be a real friend. Here everything is settled and it's all on account of you. If you can stand having these noisy young ones around you, we'd be proud to have you come and stay with us for as long as you'd like to stay. And I'm sure everybody here thinks the same."

After this long speech, Ma wiped her eyes with her apron, and looked around at her family. They were all smiling as hard as they could smile.

Mr. Jefferson scratched his chin. "It's a long time since I've lived with a family," he said, "but I'm willing to try if you are. And it wasn't all on account of me. The whole idea was Sally's, and Bill's and George's and Peter's."

Ma beamed at her family. "I always knew it was right to include the children in a family conference," she said.

4. FURNITURE, FURNITURE

NEXT MORNING, all the Parkers were up early to decide what was to be done with all their furniture. Beds, of course, had to go along, and a table and chairs. There was a kerosene stove down cellar, which Ma used sometimes on wash days. There were also some kerosene lamps, which were kept handy in case the electric lights got out of order. A small chest of drawers and some boxes to keep clothes in would be enough, and of course they could use some of the trolley car seats for living-room furniture. The children were taking some of their possessions, and Pa needed his bicycle so he could ride to town to look for a job. And then there were the kitchen utensils, Pa's tools, and a supply of boards to make shelves, and steps, and whatever was needed to make the car comfortable enough to live in.

But right away the question arose: what was to be done with the rest of the furniture? It had to be got out of the house, so the house could be rented to someone else. The children weren't much interested in furniture.

"Why don't we just sell it?" Bill asked.

"That's right," said Sally. "Then we wouldn't have to be dusting it all the time."

But Ma wouldn't hear of it. "And what will we use when we come out of the trolley car?" she asked. "You don't think we're going to stay in it the rest of our lives, do you?"

"Sure, why not?" said Bill.

"Live like gypsies!" said Ma. "Not as long as I have anything to say!"

Just then they heard the slow clop-clop of a horse outside.

"There goes Mr. Jefferson," said Sally. "Let's ask him."

"We've bothered him enough," said Pa. "You'd better leave him alone for a while."

But the horse stopped and then they heard feet clumping on the porch steps. Bill ran to open the door.

"Hello," he said to Mr. Jefferson. "You're just in time. We don't know what to do with the furniture."

"Now don't pay any attention to him," said Ma. "Sit down and have breakfast. I'm just frying some eggs."

Ma seemed to think that it was her duty to feed Mr. Jefferson every time she laid eyes on him.

"No, ma'am," he protested. "I never eat breakfast before I feed Whitey. He'll feel bad."

"I'll go out and give him some sugar," said Bill. "Please stay."

Mr. Jefferson sniffed the bacon and eggs. "All right,"

he said. "But what I really came about was the furniture."

"Oh, now don't tell us that," said Pa, "after the way Bill shouted that we didn't know what to do with it."

"I mean it," said Mr. Jefferson. "No reason why you shouldn't store it in my barn. Plenty of room in there."

"Well, I did think," said Ma, "that we could figure out a few things without bothering Mr. Jefferson. But it's such a good idea, I don't see how we can refuse. We'll do something for you sometime, Mr. Jefferson."

The rest of the day was spent in packing and moving furniture. The winter clothes were packed in a trunk with mothballs. Ma chose the dishes she would need, and the summer clothes, and the blankets and sheets, and a few bottles of medicine, just in case somebody got sick. Then Pa and Mr. Jefferson began carrying the furniture over to the barn. They took out most of the chairs and tables, and some chests of drawers. Old Whitey kept turning his head to see what was going on. He had never had tables and chairs and lamps in his house before.

"He's puzzled," said Mr. Jefferson. "He doesn't know what to make of it."

"How can you tell?" Bill asked, as they walked back to the house.

"I always know," said Mr. Jefferson.

"I suppose it's because you've lived with him such a long time," said Bill. "You get to understand him."

"Yes, that's right," said Mr. Jefferson.

Old Whitey kept turning his head to see what was going on.

Now they tackled the parlor suite. The table and the rug and the lamps were taken out. Then came the sofa. It was a big red plush sofa with carved wooden arms. It had stood in that living room ever since any of the children could remember. They had played house on it, and taken naps on it, and played Indians behind it. Mr. Jefferson and Pa lifted it and started out the door. But they didn't get far. It stuck. They turned it over. It stuck again. Pa swore at it. But that wouldn't move it. It simply would not go through the door.

"How the dickens did we ever get it in here?" Pa asked.

"I don't remember," said Ma. "It's so long ago, now, I really don't remember. The door couldn't have shrunk, could it? Or the sofa couldn't have swelled, could it?"

Pa stood and scratched his head. "I doubt it," he said. Then he grinned. "Ma," he said, "don't you remember how that door was when we moved into this house?"

Then Ma smiled. "That's so," she said. "It was a double door. And we had it made into a single door. Let in too much cold air, as I remember."

"My, that was a long time ago," said Pa. "Well, that saves us a lot of trouble. The sofa will stay here. And those two chairs, too."

"Why, what do you mean?" said Ma. "Our parlor suite that we had when we were married? You going to leave it here?"

"I certainly am," said Pa. "I always did hate the sight of that sofa, and now I'm going to get rid of it. Hooray!"

"I won't have it," said Ma.

"All right," said Pa, "if you're so set on moving it, why, you just move it, that's all."

Ma raised her eyebrows and shrugged her shoulders. She knew Pa was easy-going, but when he made up his mind about something, there wasn't any use trying to change it.

"Oh, well," she said, "I don't suppose it matters. But I never knew you didn't like it. Why on earth didn't you say so long ago?"

"Wasn't anything I could have done about it," said Pa, "especially after we got the door made smaller. But now there is something I can do about it, and so I kiss it good-by."

The children and Mr. Jefferson had stood watching and listening. They didn't mind. It was all right with them to leave the sofa behind. But now Pa and Mr. Jefferson picked up the china closet, which had been emptied of dishes and glassware. Ma was busy with something else, when suddenly she turned and saw the china closet being carried out on the porch.

"Wait," she said.

"What now?" Pa asked.

"That doesn't go in the barn," said Ma.

"Why, what are you going to do with it?" said Pa. "You want to leave this here too?"

"No," said Ma. "I am going to take it along."

"Take it along!" Pa pushed his cap on the back of his head. "Ma, have you taken leave of your senses?"

"No," said Ma, "I have not. But I'm not going to have that stored in a barn, and maybe the glass broken. I'm going to have it with me."

"Where can you put it in a trolley car?" Pa asked.

"I don't know," said Ma, "but we'll find some place for it. I got that china closet with coupons, and I don't want anything to happen to it."

"Excuse me," said Mr. Jefferson to Sally, "did she say coupons?"

"Yes," said Sally. "Soap coupons. Two thousand of them."

"Just think of all the washing I had to do to get that china closet," said Ma. "Two thousand cakes of soap!"

As she stood there in the middle of the room with her hands on her hips, they could tell that she wasn't going to give in about that china closet.

"All right," Pa said.

5. ALL ABOARD!

THE NEXT DAY was Friday, and the last day of school. Sally and Bill and George had to go to get their report cards, and to say good-by to all their friends, and explain that they were moving. All the other children envied them. They could hardly believe that the Parker children could be so lucky. The Parker children could hardly believe it either, but they had no time to stop and think about it. As soon as school was out they had to run home and help with the packing and the cleaning up. And they all had to go to bed very early.

At the crack of dawn next day all the Parkers were up. This was the great day. Right after breakfast all of them got busy. They piled all the things that were to go in the trolley car on the front porch. Then Mr. Parker went around to the car barn for the last time to get the car.

On the other side of the fence Mr. Jefferson was busy too, locking up his house, hitching up Whitey, and tying the other horse to the back of his milk wagon. He had all his clothes and things in the wagon, which was to be hitched on behind when the time came for the horses to pull the car. Bill was helping him.

Mrs. Parker had some large baskets packed with enough provisions to last for several days, until they could find out where to do their shopping. She was putting the last of the breakfast things into a basket. Sally was sweeping the empty rooms. Peter was trotting around, very much surprised at the amount of space in the house.

"Clang! Clang!" went a bell outside.

"Children!" Mrs. Parker called. "There's your father!"

"We're coming, Pa!" the children called.

Sally finished her sweeping and put the broom out on the porch. Bill and Mr. Jefferson hurried over to help load things in the car. The china closet was put on the back landing with the kerosene stove. Mattresses were spread across the car seats. Suitcases and boxes were put under the seats. They had to work fast so as to get out of the way before the next car should come along. Pa had arranged with the car company to allow him some time to get started, but still they had to hurry.

Ma put Peter on one of the mattresses. He couldn't understand why they were making all this fuss about going on a picnic, or why he had such a nice soft seat all to himself, but it was all right with him.

Bill got up in front with his father.

Mr. Jefferson climbed into his wagon.

"Where's George?" said Sally. George wasn't to be seen.

"Where is that child?" Ma exclaimed. "He's the biggest slowpoke I ever saw in my life. Georgie!"

Just then George's voice called, "Ma, look what I found!" There he was sticking his head out of the attic window, waving a large birdcage. "Can I take it?"

"Certainly not," said his mother. "You come right down." She went back inside to get him. "I'll just make sure the windows are all locked, while I'm there," she said. They could hear the noise of a window being banged down, and Ma's footsteps echoing through the empty house. Pretty soon she came out on the porch, holding George as if she thought he might disappear. George still had the birdcage. Ma locked the door, and both climbed into the car.

"Now can we yell good-by to the house?" George asked.

"Can I clang the bell now?" said Bill.

"No, indeed," said Ma. "Everybody in the whole street is asleep. It's only six o'clock. No shouting!"

"Can't I clang the bell even once?" Bill begged.

"All right," said Pa. "I guess they won't notice that." So Bill put his foot on the button.

"Clang!" went the bell. The children waved good-by, and Pa started the car. Mr. Jefferson followed, driving his milk wagon.

The children ran up and down inside the trolley car, buzzed the bells, and waved out of the windows to Mr. Jefferson.

In nearly all the houses, the shades were still down. There were very few people in the streets. One or two early risers stared out of their windows to see a street car loaded with furniture, and a milk wagon with one horse in front and another behind. And a couple of times working men waiting at the street corners for a trolley car were astonished when Mr. Parker didn't stop and let them get aboard.

But for the most part they were not noticed. In less than two hours they were at the end of the line.

Now it was time to hitch up the horses. Pa got out and unhitched the trolley from the wire. Mr. Jefferson tied the wagon on behind the car, and hitched the horses on in front, and they started out on the old track. It was rusty. Weeds grew between the rails. Now and then a rabbit jumped out of the way. The wheels made a terrible grating noise. They had to go slowly.

An automobile passed them on the dirt road that ran alongside the track. The driver turned and stared at them. They passed farmhouses. People came out and stared.

"What are they looking at?" said Sally.

"Us," said Pa. "There hasn't been a car on this track in fifteen years."

"Giddap," said Mr. Jefferson to the horses. But they

couldn't giddap any faster. They had to pick their way among the weeds and stones.

At lunch time Mr. Jefferson unhitched the horses and turned them loose to graze. Ma brought out sandwiches and milk. After lunch Peter was put to sleep on his mattress in the car.

"Now," said Pa, "I wonder where we are. I think I'll go and ask that farmhouse yonder."

Bill went along with Pa. Sally helped her mother clear up the remains of lunch, Mr. Jefferson sat under a tree and smoked a pipe, and George lay down beside Peter and went to sleep too.

In half an hour Pa and Bill came back. Ma watched them coming across the field.

"What in the world have they got there?" said Ma, shading her eyes with her hand. "Well, I do declare! Chickens!"

"Look, Ma!" Bill called, as they came nearer.

"Where'd you get them?" said Ma. "And what are we going to do with them?"

"Bought 'em," said Pa, proudly. He held a gray and white speckled hen by the legs, and Bill struggled with a black hen. "Don't let that hen go, Bill," said Pa.

Mr. Jefferson came and felt of the black one. "Nice bird," he said. He didn't look surprised. Nothing the Parkers did surprised him any more.

"Bought the two of them for a dollar," said Pa. "Now maybe we'll get some eggs."

"Why, Pa, what a wonderful idea," said Sally. "But where will we keep them right now? They'll fly out of the windows."

"Cut, cut, cut," said the speckled hen, angrily.

"Squawk!" went the black one.

"I know," said Bill, "that birdcage of Georgie's." He went and got it out of the car and they stuffed the fowls into it. It was a tight squeeze, but Bill kept telling them they wouldn't have to stay there long. The black hen pecked at him angrily through the bars.

"All right, let's get going," said Pa. "The lady at that farm said this is eight miles from Taylorville. Our place is five miles from Taylorville, so we have three miles to go. I hope we know the place when we see it."

"There's a red painted barn, you said," said Mr. Jefferson.

"Yes," said Pa, "with a big picture of a bull on it, for Bull Durham tobacco. And across the road is a yellow farmhouse. Now everybody keep watch for those landmarks."

The horses plodded on. The wheels scraped on the tracks. The hens complained from their cage, and Peter and George slept peacefully.

At last Bill and Sally, who were stationed as lookouts, one on each side of the car, called out, "There it is!" On one side of the road was the yellow farmhouse. On the other was a level field. There had once been a wire fence separating the field from the road, but the wire was gone and only the fence posts remained, sticking up crookedly out of the ground. A lane led back from the road to a barn which had once been red but was now a rusty brown. The faded picture of a big bull could still be seen on one wall.

"Whoa!" said Mr. Jefferson. The horses stopped, and the wheels gave one last groan and were silent.

Sally and Bill climbed down and looked around. Ma and Pa and Mr. Jefferson climbed down. It was quiet and hot in the afternoon sun. Suddenly George woke up. The car had stopped. He was all alone with Peter. Still half asleep, he staggered to the door and climbed down.

"Did we get here?" he yawned. "Hey, what are you doing with my birdcage?"

"We got some chickens," said Bill. "You were asleep. Pa, what do I do with these chickens now? Can I let them out of the cage?"

"No, no," said Sally, "they'll get away."

George yawned again. "Tie them with a string," he said.

"That's a good idea," said Pa. He pulled a ball of string out of his pocket and gave it to Bill. Bill tied a long piece to each bird's leg and fastened the ends to the wheel of the trolley car. The hens walked around, pecking at the ground and making clucking noises.

"Soon as we get settled I'll make a house for them," said Bill.

"I wonder where the house was on this farm," said Sally. "Maybe over there where those trees are." She pointed to a grove of trees off to the right of the barn. Back of the barn was a low hill, which seemed to be covered with bushes and young trees.

"Maybe up on the hill," said George.

"What do we do now?" Bill asked.

Pa and Mr. Jefferson were busy unhitching the horses and turning them into the field to graze. But Ma seemed at a loss. She was usually so busy that she didn't have time to stand around. And now here she was in the middle of a field with nothing to do.

Suddenly Peter began to cry. He got up on his knees on his mattress and looked out of the window and howled.

"Dinner!" he yelled.

If this was a picnic, he wanted to eat.

"Well, the poor thing," said Mrs. Parker. "He's hungry. And you must all be hungry, and here I am standing and doing nothing!"

At once she began to be busy.

"Now the first thing to do is to make a fire so I can get some supper together. You boys go up on that hill back of the barn and find some wood. And Sally, you start unpacking the basket and get out the bowls and bread and butter."

As soon as Ma started giving orders, everybody began to move. Pa found some big stones to make a fire-place. In a little while Bill came back with his arms full of wood. Pa made a fire, and put a big pot on a gridiron across the fireplace.

"Here, Mr. Jefferson," said Ma. "You might open some cans of soup. Eating three meals a day is such a nuisance, it's a good thing we like it, or maybe we'd just eat grass like the horses."

"I wouldn't want to just eat grass, Mama," said Bill.

"Well, it would save me a lot of trouble if you did," said Ma. But she didn't look as if she meant it. "Now, Sally, keep Peter out of the fire, like a good girl."

In a short time a tablecloth was spread out, and bowls of hot soup were ready. There was sliced ham too, and potato salad, and baked beans, and milk, and chocolate cake.

The two hens got as close to the feast as their strings would allow.

"The poor creatures are hungry," said Ma. "What did you plan to feed them, Pa?"

"Well, I didn't think much about it," said Pa. "I thought I'd get some chicken feed in town."

"Better give them some bread in the meantime," said Ma. "It may be some time before you get to town. Now we're all ready. Is everybody here?"

"Where's George?" Sally asked. George was not to be seen.

"I thought that he went up the hill with you, Bill," said Ma.

"Sure," said Bill. "I thought he went up for more wood."

"George!" they all shouted. "George!"

"I'm coming," a faint voice answered. Down the lane

from the barn came a bedraggled figure. He was dripping wet.

"Where have you been?" Ma demanded. "What I'm going to do with that child I don't know. How'd you get so wet?"

George wiped his face with his sleeve. "I fell in the water," he said.

"Water! What water?"

"I don't know," said George. "There's a brook or something up on that hill behind the barn."

"Brook on top of a hill? I never heard of such a thing."

"It's not exactly on top," George began.

"Must be a spring," Pa said. "This was a farm; farm has to have water. What did it look like, Georgie?"

Ma clucked her tongue impatiently. "Now don't stop to ask him questions," she said. "I've got to get dry clothes on him. You people go ahead and eat your soup while I change George."

She pushed him ahead of her into the trolley car. There she opened the first suitcase she came to. "Take those wet things off, George," she said. "Hurry, now. Oh, dear, these aren't your clothes. They're Papa's. Well, it can't be helped. They'll do to bundle you up in while we eat our supper."

When George descended the steps of the car, trailing Pa's shirt tails behind him, his family took one look, and then laughed so hard that they almost spilled their soup.

"That's all right," said Ma. "I had to take the first

The beds were made across the seats.

things I could find. Somehow George always has to find out about things the hardest way he can."

After supper, Ma said, "Now I think we're all so tired that we ought to go to bed as soon as we can."

"That's right," said Pa.

The children didn't think it a very good idea. Sally, being the oldest, thought she ought to stay up later, and Bill wanted a game of baseball, and George wanted to go up the hill again and show where he had fallen into the water. However, Pa and Mr. Jefferson got to work pulling everything out of the car except the mattresses. The beds were made across the seats, and Ma opened another suitcase, the right one this time, and found pajamas.

"Now we won't even brush our teeth," she said. "We'll do it tomorrow when we have fresh water."

"I could get some," said George.

"In the morning," said Ma, firmly, "we'll go up there and see what sort of water you discovered, and if it's fit to use we'll use it. If not, we'll find out from that farmhouse yonder where good water is to be had. Also milk. Now you'd better get to bed, all you children."

The children curled up on their mattresses, and were soon asleep, even George, who had had a nap.

The grownups sat beside the fire a little longer. It was a fine evening. The western sky was red with the sunset, and one star twinkled in the blue overhead.

"Well, Mr. Jefferson," said Ma, "how do you like staying awake all day?"

"Fine," said Mr. Jefferson. "And the funny thing is, I'm not tired. Feel as if I could go right to work."

"Well," said Pa, "I feel as if I could go right to bed. And I think you will too, pretty soon."

Mr. Jefferson yawned. "Maybe you're right," he said. "I'll just take the horses up the hill for a drink, seeing George found the water, and then I'll see how it feels to sleep all night."

6. THE PERKINSES

SALLY WAS the first to awaken the next morning. Sunlight streamed through the windows of the trolley car. At first she didn't know what had waked her or where she was. Her room at home was on the north side, and was never very bright in the morning. She sat up and looked around. Why, of course! They were out in the country, sleeping in the trolley car! There were Bill and George, sound asleep. There was Peter, rolled up in his blanket. There were her father and mother, and off at the other end of the car, Mr. Jefferson. His straw hat hung on the end of the seat nearest him.

Suddenly Bill's head popped up. He blinked his eyes, looked all around, and then sat up. Sally could see that he didn't know where he was. Then he saw Sally. He stared at her. Then he grinned. Sally pointed silently to the door. Bill nodded. Then they both got into their clothes, quickly, without making a sound, and taking their shoes in their hands, they tiptoed down the steps. They sat down and put their shoes on.

It was a beautiful sunny morning. The two horses were eating grass not far away. The hens were scratching in the dirt for bugs.

The trolley car shone bright yellow in the sunshine, and across the road was the farmhouse, yellow too, though not as bright as the car. A lane led from the road back to the house. Off to one side of the house were the barns. Some cows grazed in a field nearby.

A woman came out of the barn, with a pail in her hand, and walked to the house.

"My, they get up early over there," said Sally. "What do you think she has in the pail?"

"Milk," said Bill. "I guess they just got through milking. I wonder if they have any kids."

"Let's go across the road where we can see better," said Sally. "I think I saw a girl come out on the porch. It would be fun if they have a girl over there."

"Oh, a girl," said Bill, scornfully. "What I'd like to know is, have they got any boys?"

Sally glared at her brother. "Goodness knows," she said, "there are enough boys around here. It would be nice to have a girl for a change."

They walked across to the fence that separated the front yard from the road. On the other side of the fence were some lilac bushes.

"Come on over here where there aren't any bushes," said Bill.

At that, the bushes began to shake and rustle.

"Sh! There's somebody there," Sally whispered.

There was a giggle, a low growl, and then somebody said, "Quiet, Rex!"

"Who's in there?" Bill demanded.

The bushes parted and out stepped a boy with very light yellow hair. He was wearing faded blue overalls, and with one hand he held the collar of a big brown dog.

"Where'd you come from?" he asked.

"We just moved out here," said Bill.

"Where's your house?"

"Over there," said Bill, pointing to the trolley.

The boy stared at the car. Then he stared at Sally and Bill. Then he said, "Come on out, Martha."

A little girl with brown curls came out from behind the bushes and stared too. She twisted one of her curls in her fingers and peeped out from behind her brother.

"She doesn't say much," said the boy. "She's bashful. What's your names?"

"I'm Bill Parker, and this is Sally," said Bill. "What's yours?"

"Tom," said the boy. "Tom Perkins. How'd you get here? And what do you mean that's your house? That's no house."

"Well, it's a trolley car," said Sally. "But just the same, we're going to live in it. Us, and our father and mother, and two brothers, and Mr. Jefferson. He's the milkman. We've got two horses, that towed the car out here."

"Jumping grasshoppers!" said the boy. "Wait till I tell Aunt Hannah!"

"Where's your father and mother?" Sally asked.

"We haven't got any mother," said the boy. "We live with Aunt Hannah Perkins. Our father's on a ship."

Just then they heard the tinkle of a bell.

"That's the breakfast bell," said the boy. "Come on, Martha!" And they both turned and started toward the house with the dog after them.

Halfway to the house, the boy turned around. "Say!" he said. "You folks need anything? Milk, or something like that?"

Sally and Bill looked at each other, and nodded. "Yes, we do," said Sally.

"Well, come up to the house. Aunt Hannah'll fix you up."

Sally and Bill followed Tom to the house and into the kitchen. A pleasant-looking lady in a pink gingham dress and a white apron stood at the stove frying pancakes.

Martha had gotten there ahead of them, and she was pouring milk from a pitcher into the glasses on the table. She looked at them shyly, and then quickly looked down at the pitcher again.

Tom burst out, "Aunt Hannah, look who's here! They're from across the road, and they came in the trolley car last night, and they're going to *live* in it!"

"Live in it! What fun!" said Aunt Hannah.

"I'm Sally Parker and this is Bill," Sally said. "We came across the road to get a look at your place."

Martha giggled. "And they came over to the fence and there we were on the other side of it, and Rex growled at them!"

"Well, I'm glad to have that trolley car explained to me," said Aunt Hannah. "There hasn't been a car on that track for fifteen years. I came in from milking yesterday, and there was the car, and I thought I was seeing things. Then I said to the children, 'I guess they're going to start using that old line again.'"

"We thought it would be a good way for us to get to school in the winter," said Tom.

"Oh, where do you go to school?" Sally asked.

"Taylorville," said Tom. "Five miles from here."

"Then this morning," Aunt Hannah went on, "the car was still there. So right after milking Tom had to get a look at it. That's why he and Martha were hiding behind those bushes."

"Do you *milk?*" Bill exclaimed.

"Sure, why not," said Tom, scornfully. "Oh, Aunt Hannah, by the way, can they have some milk?"

"Of course," said Aunt Hannah. "With children in the family you must want milk. I'll go and get some. No, wait. You two sit down and have breakfast. Or have you had yours?"

"No, we haven't," said Sally, "but we really ought to go back. Ma will be up and she'll be wondering where we are."

But Bill's mouth was watering at the sight and smell of the pancakes. He was very hungry. Aunt Hannah looked at him, and the corners of her mouth went up just a little.

"Oh, it won't take long," she said. "You sit down and begin, while I make some more. Your mother will think you've gone exploring. And so you have."

And she flipped two pancakes onto each plate, and poured more batter onto the griddle.

The four children sat down and attacked their pancakes, and between bites, Sally explained everything from the beginning—about Mr. Jefferson, and Pa's losing his job and asking for the car, and how they thought of renting the land and towing the car out here, and everything.

Aunt Hannah said, "That's the best story I've heard in years. I must come and visit you. If I'd thought there were people staying there I would have come over last night. You tell your mother to let me know if there's anything she wants."

When the pancakes were all gone, and the last drop of maple syrup cleaned up, Sally got up.

"Thank you for the pancakes," she said politely. "I think we'd better go now. They'll be sending George to look for us, and then something will be sure to happen to him. That's our brother," she explained. "He always has something happen to him. Yesterday he fell into some water up on the hill and got all wet. We don't know what the water was but we're going to explore and find out."

Tom said, "Oh, that must be the spring."

"You mean there's a spring up there!" Bill exclaimed. "Boy, that's wonderful. Let's tell Pa!"

"Sure," said Tom. "Good spring water. Must be full of leaves, though. You'll have to clean it out."

"Have you been over there?" said Sally.

"Sure," said Tom. "Been all around. Good barn they have up there. Going to fall down, though, if somebody doesn't take care of it. Got stalls for horses and stanchions for cows. Say, you want to see our cows? And I'll show you my calf. She's two days old."

He jumped up, ready to take his guests on a tour. But Aunt Hannah put her hand on his arm.

"Maybe not right now," she said. "Sally and Bill have to get back. But they'll come again."

"You bet we will," said Bill. "Boy! I wish we had a cow! All we have is two hens. And the horses. But of course Mr. Jefferson is going to take them back when his vacation is over."

Martha shyly whispered something in her aunt's ear.

"Maybe so," Aunt Hannah answered. "Martha says maybe you people would like one of our kittens. We have three, and they're old enough to leave their mother now."

"Oh, I'd *love* one," said Sally. "Could we see them?"

"No, come on home," said Bill, grabbing her arm.

"I know what you mean," Aunt Hannah told him. "Once a couple of girls get mooning over some kittens, and trying to decide which is the prettiest, there's no getting them away. Well, here's your milk. And here's

something else your mother might like." And she handed
Bill the pail of milk, and Sally a pan covered with a napkin.

Sally said "Thank you," but Bill lifted the napkin and
peeped underneath. It was a pie, with a big C cut in the
golden brown crust.

"Oh, boy!" Bill sighed. "That sure looks good. Wait
till Ma sees it. And wait till she sees this milk! Say!" he
said to Tom. "You'd better come over and see us."

"Okay," said Tom, "soon as I get my work done."

"Tom is the man around here," said Aunt Hannah,
putting her arm around his shoulders. "He helps me run
the farm. But we'll be over later."

"Me too," said Martha, smiling at Sally.

7. A HOME IN THE WILDERNESS

WHEN SALLY and Bill got back to the trolley car, they found the family up. Pa was feeding the fire with some wood that George had just brought. Ma was frying bacon and eggs, and Mr. Jefferson was sitting on the steps of the car with Peter on his lap. Peter had just grabbed Mr. Jefferson's straw hat and was putting it on his own head, which it covered like a bushel basket. Mr. Jefferson was looking a little scared, as if this was the first time a small boy had ever sat on his lap.

"Well, where have *you* been?" Ma exclaimed, looking up from her cooking. "Aren't you hungry? The idea of gallivanting off at this time of the morning without saying a word!"

"You were asleep, Ma," said Sally. "We didn't want to wake you. We went across the road to get a good look at the farmhouse—"

"And we saw the boy and girl that live there, and their aunt, and look what they gave us!" Bill burst out.

Ma stood up and looked. "Well, I declare!" she exclaimed. "Milk! Why, that's wonderful! We actually have neighbors way out here in the wilderness! And what smart children you are! But I hope you thanked the lady politely—"

Pa interrupted: "Of course we have neighbors, Ma. This isn't a wilderness. It's only five miles away from the town."

"Well, it feels like a wilderness to me," said Ma. "But what's this?"

Sally held out the pie to her. "They gave us this too. They thought you might like it."

Her mother lifted the napkin and stared at the pie. "Well, that settles it," she exclaimed. "Now I *know* we're in civilized country. I was beginning to feel like a gypsy, cooking over an open fire. But if there's folks here that can bake pies, and put a C on them, and I guess that means Cherry, then it's all right. And as soon as I can get my stove set up I'm going to make a nice cake and send it over. Sally, I hope you asked the lady to come and visit us."

"Yes, Ma—"

"I hope," Pa interrupted, "that she'll come soon, so you can see we aren't among the heathen."

But Ma ignored his remark. "Now come and have breakfast, everybody," she said. "We've got to fix this place up, if we're going to live in it and have visitors. Sally and Bill, come and sit down."

"We had breakfast," said Sally.

"You *had!* Heavens!" said Ma. "How many times have I told you children not to go into anyone's house when they're eating?"

"But, Ma," Bill protested. "Tom told us to come and get some milk, and we thought you'd want some for Peter, and there was his Aunt Hannah making pancakes —we couldn't just walk out!"

George said under his breath, "You could have grabbed a couple of pancakes for me!" But fortunately Ma didn't hear him.

The family sat in a semi-circle, and Ma went from one to the other, dishing out bacon and eggs.

"How'd you sleep last night, Mr. Jefferson?" Pa inquired.

"Fine, fine," said Mr. Jefferson. He had a piece of bread in one hand and a cup of coffee in the other. His straw hat was on the back of his head, and he sat cross-legged on the ground. Suddenly, his face wrinkled up, just as it had a few days ago when he was looking at the Parker family across the fence. His mouth stretched and the corners turned up, and he grinned. Then he made a curious sound.

"Ha!" he said.

It was a laugh. It sounded a bit rusty, but it certainly was a laugh. The Parkers all turned and stared at him.

"I was just thinking," said Mr. Jefferson, "how surprised I would have been a week ago if I could have seen myself now!"

"No more than any of us," George piped up.

"Georgie!" his mother said. "I don't know what to do with that boy. He'll sit quiet as a mouse, and then when he does speak he'll say the wrong thing. Don't listen to him, Mr. Jefferson."

"That's all right," said Mr. Jefferson. "He didn't mean any harm."

"Whether he did or not," said Ma, "he's got to learn to look before he leaps. Now look at the way he fell into the water last night."

"Oh!" said Bill. "That reminds me. That boy Tom said it's a spring. And his aunt said so too. So if it's spring water, we can drink it, can't we?"

"A spring!" said Pa. "Well, now if everybody's finished—" and he stood up and wiped his mustache—"I want to have a look at that water, or spring, or whatever it is. And we'll have to look at the barn too. The boys can go with me."

"Sally, you stay here," said her mother. "I need you to help me."

"Maybe I can do something around the house too," said Mr. Jefferson. "I'm used to housekeeping."

"Well, there's plenty to do," said Ma. "But what shall we do with Peter while we work? Sally will have to mind him."

"Oh, Ma, I want to help too," Sally complained.

"No, he'll run into the road," said Ma.

Mr. Jefferson's eye fell on the hens, pecking about under the car.

"Tie him to a wheel," he suggested.

"That's a good idea," said Ma. "Sally, go and get the clothesline. It's packed in the wash basket with the clothespins."

Peter didn't mind a bit being tied up like the chickens. He got down under the car and called to them. "Here chicken, here nice chicken." The chickens, however, squawked and flapped their wings and got as far away from him as their strings would allow.

Sally got a piece of bread and gave it to Peter.

"Give the chickens some bread," she told him. She threw down a crumb to show him how, and the black hen snapped it up. Then Peter threw down a crumb and the speckled hen got it. Then he decided to eat the rest himself.

Ma gave him a pan and a spoon to dig with and he sat in the shade, digging and talking happily to the chickens.

Ma and Sally and Mr. Jefferson then surveyed the car.

"Now," said Ma, "the way I see it, we'll have the kitchen on the back platform. Let's set up the stove first of all, right across from the doorway. Then if we don't get another thing done, at least I can cook some food without squatting over a camp fire."

After the stove was set up and the tank filled with kerosene, Ma looked at the motorman's box. There was no way to get rid of it.

"Let's use it for a kitchen table," said Sally.

"That's a good idea," her mother said, "only it's not big enough."

"Haven't we got some lumber?" Mr. Jefferson asked. "We could build a shelf on top of the box, right across the width of the car. Then you'll have all the working surface you need."

"And you can sit on the motorman's stool," Sally cried. She ran to the front end of the car and pulled up the stool, on which Pa had sat for so many years.

"Won't Pa be surprised!" she said, as she fitted the iron pipe into the hole in the floor.

Mr. Jefferson sawed off two lengths of board for his shelf and nailed them in place, while Ma hammered in nails up and down the window frames to hang her pots and pans.

Then Sally arranged her mother's bright blue and yellow canisters along the back of the shelf. The boxes of groceries were stowed underneath, as well as the dishpans and water bucket.

"We can set up our table outdoors for today," said Ma. "Now I've got the kitchen fixed so I can cook in it, I'll just step down out of the car door to serve the food. Then when Pa comes back we can unscrew the seats so we can put furniture inside. But I think we've done enough for this morning. I must say it looks right nice and cheerful. I always did want a kitchen with a lot of windows so I could look out. And this one is so small, I can sit right on that stool and reach everything in it."

While she talked, she put some potatoes in a pot and set them on the stove to boil.

"I hope they bring back some water," she said. "This is the last of what we have."

Mr. Jefferson lifted the table down to the ground, and meanwhile Sally got benches and chairs and set them around.

"You might as well set the table, Sally," Ma called, handing down a tablecloth. "My land, what's that hen making all the noise about?"

The black hen was clucking excitedly, walking back and forth with her wings spread.

The speckled hen continued to peck for bugs, and paid no attention to her excited sister.

"I guess I'll call the black one Mrs. Cluck," Sally said, "and the other one Mrs. Peck. Though I wish I could see what Mrs. Cluck is clucking about. Are you bothering the chicken, Peter?"

Peter came out from under the car, trailing his rope, and stood watching Sally set the table.

"Dinner," he said, with a pleased smile on his little round face. He waddled to the table and put a round brown object on it.

"Yes, honey, you'll have dinner soon," said Sally. "Now don't put stones on the table." Then she stopped and stared. It wasn't a stone. It was an egg! A beautiful, smooth, brown egg!

"Mama!" Sally called. "Mr. Jefferson! Look! An egg! Mrs. Cluck laid it. That's what she was clucking about!"

"An egg!" said her mother. "What are you talking about, child?"

"Peter found an egg! Mrs. Cluck laid it. The black hen!"

"Well, for goodness sake!" said Ma. "Bring it in here. We won't eat it, that's sure. At least, not for a while.

I'll boil it and we'll put it in the china closet, as soon as we get it set up in the right place. And we must get some chicken feed, if the hens are going to lay. Well, that makes me feel good! To have the stove set up and the hen lay an egg!" And she popped it into the water with the potatoes to cook.

8. EXPLORATION AND DISCOVERY

W HILE SALLY and Mr. Jefferson and Mrs. Parker were rearranging the car, Mr. Parker and
Bill and George were busy exploring. They had
taken a couple of pails for water, and a big shovel in
case they should have to dig. They started along the
lane that led from the road back to the barn.

"The water I fell into was sort of up that hill," said
George, pointing off to one side of the barn.

"Well, we'll investigate the barn first," said Pa.

The grass grew high in the deserted barnyard. An
old watering trough stood under the eaves. Pa and the
boys walked through the weeds and pushed the door
open. It creaked on its rusty hinges. A bird, startled at
the noise, flew out from under the roof.

It was cool inside, after the hot sunshine outdoors.
Weeds grew up through the cracks in the wooden floor.
There were stalls for horses and cows along the sides.
There was still hay in the hayloft above their heads.

At the end opposite the door was a small room fenced

"It's rusty, but it's still good."

off with a high wooden wall. Pa opened the door and they went in. A little door led to the outside.

"What was this room for?" Bill asked.

"Pigs, maybe," said Pa. He was poking in a corner at a big thing made of rusty iron.

"What's that?" George asked.

"It's a plow," said his father. "It's rusty, but it's still good." He dragged it out into the middle of the floor. The three of them stood and looked down at the plow. Then all three had the same idea at the same time.

"We could have a garden!" they said.

"It's late for a garden," Pa said. "But maybe we could still plant something."

"Corn would be nice," said George.

"Well, we'll think about it," Pa said. He turned to go. But Bill had noticed something else.

"Pa, I don't think there were pigs here," he said. "Look at all these boxes nailed to the wall."

"Why, those are nests for chickens," said Pa. "I guess they kept the chickens in here."

"That's right," Bill cried. "And that little door is for them to go out. Why couldn't we put our chickens in here?"

"And here's some old chicken wire," said George. "We could make a fence outside so they couldn't get away."

Pa examined the rusty tangled old wire. "It's not much good," he said. "Still, we could use it and buy some more. This wouldn't be enough."

They went back into the main part of the barn, and Pa examined the horse stalls. The mangers were chewed and bitten, but the doors were all strong.

"It's a good old barn," said Pa. "We'll put the horses in here tonight. I'd like to see all those stalls full of animals. Like when I was a boy. Hear the chickens clucking, and the cows mooing!"

He sighed and shook his head. "Well, we won't talk about that now. Let's see that water you fell into yesterday, George."

They went out into the sun again, and George led the way up the slope through tangled weeds and blackberry brambles.

Way off to the right was the grove of trees they had seen from the road. Flocks of birds were flying in and out among the trees, making a great noise.

"Look, Pa," said George, stopping and pointing. "Look at all those birds! Let's go and see what's making them so excited."

"No," said Pa. "We came to investigate that water you fell into. And don't you go off anywhere and get into any more trouble. We'll see about the birds later."

"Better hold him, Pa," Bill advised, "or he'll fall into a bed of poison ivy or a nest of rattlesnakes."

"Okay," said George, going on up the hill. He poked around in the grass and then stopped. "Here it is. See why I fell in?"

"I see," said Pa. "It's so overgrown with weeds, I'd have to fall in myself to find it."

A trickle of water seemed to be coming right up out of the ground and flowing away into the grass. Pa pushed away the grass with his shovel. He stuck the shovel in and dug out a lot of dead leaves. He dug and he dug till he came to some sand. The water was muddy from his digging, but Pa stood up and looked pleased.

Bill and George got down on their knees and put their hands in. "Oh, boy!" said Bill. "It's cold! Can I drink some?"

"Wait till the mud settles," said Pa. "It's a spring.

He dug and he dug.

There's no better water than spring water. It must be good because it's coming right up out of the ground. Now after the mud settles, that will be as clear as the water that used to come out of the tap at home."

He went on digging till he had cleared a little round basin. The water bubbled up and soon filled the basin. Bill sat down on the ground to wait for the water to clear. Suddenly, plop! A little green frog jumped out of the grass right into the water, and sat there.

"Hey, Pa!" Bill exclaimed. "A frog! Get him out!"

"That's all right, Bill," said Pa. "He won't hurt anything. He'll help keep the water clean."

After a while, the water looked pretty clear, and Pa filled the buckets.

"Let's go back now," he said. "There's plenty more work to be done. Where's George?"

Bill looked around. "I don't know," he said. "He was right here a minute ago."

"George!" Pa shouted. "Oh, George! Come on, we're going now." Nobody answered.

"Now where did that boy go to?" said Pa, impatiently. "Can't sit still for a minute, and always into something."

"Maybe he went down there where those trees are," said Bill. "He wanted to see the birds. I'll go and look for him."

Bill ran across the field to the trees, then he turned and waved.

"Come on, Pa!" he yelled. "Bring a pail and come quick!"

Pa couldn't think what Bill was so excited about. He quickly emptied the water out of one of his pails and ran across the field. When he got to the clump of trees, both boys were gone.

"Where are you?" he called.

"We're up in a tree!" Bill shouted. "Come on, Pa! Did you bring a pail?"

Pa craned his neck to see what his sons were doing up in the tree. "Yes, I brought a pail," he said crossly. "What for?"

"Cherries!" said Bill. "Millions of 'em."

"We can't get down!" said George. "We've got our hands full. MMM, they're good!"

"I thought something had happened to you," said Pa. "Didn't I tell you not to go anywhere? Now you come right down, before I get mad."

"But Pa," George protested, "you can't get mad. Just hold up the pail so I can drop the cherries in. The birds were eating them all up."

"Well, all right," said Pa.

"There's an awful lot here," said Bill, picking as fast as he could. "Wait till Ma sees them. Will she be glad!"

When the pail was half full, Bill handed it down to Pa, and then both boys climbed down. Their faces and hands were red with cherry juice.

Pa was looking up at another tree. "This looks like a pear tree," he said. "Though I don't see any pears on it. And over here's an apple tree. Georgie, I guess you found the orchard."

"I didn't know it was an orchard," said George. "I just saw all those birds flying around, and hollering to

"Cherries! Millions of 'em!

each other, and then I saw the cherries in the tree, so I climbed up."

"Well, that's fine," said Pa, eating a handful of cherries. "Only we'll have to make a rule. No eating anything you find around here on trees or anywhere else, unless a grown-up says you can. Understand?"

"But why not, Pa?" Bill asked. "What's the matter with cherries?"

"Cherries are all right," said Pa. "But something might look like cherries to you, and you might get sick. You kids aren't used to the country. Now don't forget."

"Okay, Pa," said George. "But it was all right this time."

"It was fine, this time," said Pa. "If we can get these trees cleaned up, we might have some fruit. They need pruning, and spraying, and cultivating—there certainly is a lot of work to be done around here."

"Well, come on," said Bill, picking up the pail of cherries. "I bet Ma will be surprised when she sees these."

"Maybe she'll make us another pie!" said George.

9. A BUSY AFTERNOON

DINNER THAT day was a lively meal. The barn explorers had so much to tell, and the trolley car workers had so many plans to discuss, that it seemed as if they would sit there all day and not do anything.

Everybody was pleased to eat from a table again, and even the children, though they thought the camp fire was fun, agreed that Ma's food tasted better when cooked on a stove. As Peter's high chair had been left behind, he had to sit on somebody's lap. He seemed to prefer Mr. Jefferson's.

"Peter, leave Mr. Jefferson alone," said Ma.

But Mr. Jefferson shook his head and said, "He's all right. He can sit here and look at my medal. I bet you folks never knew I had a medal."

"A medal!" said George. "Were you in the army?"

"No," said Mr. Jefferson. "I got it from the milk company." He pulled the end of his gold watch chain out of its vest pocket, and there on the end of it dangled a gold medal! He held it up for the Parkers to see. On one side was a picture of a milk wagon engraved in the gold. On the other was some writing.

George took the medal in his hand and read: "To Augustus Jefferson, on the completion of ten years of faithful service."

"My goodness," said Sally. "I never knew a milk company would give you a medal for delivering milk!"

"They don't all do it," said Mr. Jefferson. "This milk company is special."

"I guess they figure," said Pa, "that anybody who gets up in the middle of the night to deliver milk is a hero."

"*We* should give Mr. Jefferson a medal too," said George, "for lending us his horse to get out here. Gosh! If it hadn't been for him, we wouldn't have had all those cherries!"

"I suppose you think," said his mother, "that it was worthwhile for Pa to lose his job and for us all to move, just so you could get enough cherries!"

"Yes," said George, counting the cherry pits on his plate. "Mr. Jefferson, I wish you didn't have to go back to your job. Why don't you just stay here with us?"

Suddenly Mr. Jefferson's pleasant expression changed. He scowled and looked very cross.

"Wish I could," he muttered. "But I can't."

"Now we won't talk about that any more," said Ma. "I don't want anybody to mention it. It just makes Mr. Jefferson feel bad."

"I never knew your name was Augustus," said Sally, tactfully changing the subject.

"Why didn't they call you Thomas?" Bill asked. "Then you could be Thomas Jefferson."

"I guess they didn't want to mix me up with the first Thomas Jefferson," said Mr. Jefferson. "They called me Augustus because I was born in August."

"Well," said George, "if you stay until August, we can have a birthday party, and Ma will bake you a cake."

"George!" said Ma. "I said we wouldn't talk about that. Now you keep still."

George was quiet. So was everybody else. But it was easier to keep from talking about Mr. Jefferson's going back than from thinking about it. They all felt sad, except Peter, who sat playing with the medal, putting it into the pocket and taking it out again, and occasionally putting it in his mouth to see how it tasted.

After a while Pa said, "I think we should go to Taylorville soon. We need supplies."

"That's true," said Ma. "Flour, and soap, and some fresh vegetables, and yeast, so I can make bread."

"Well, we'd better go tomorrow," said Pa, "and bring the things home in the wagon. We won't be able to do it when Mr. Jefferson takes the horses away."

"Pa!" said George reproachfully. "I thought we weren't going to talk about that!"

Pa looked very much ashamed of himself. He didn't know what to say. But little Peter saved the situation by falling asleep in Mr. Jefferson's lap. He had found that by leaning his head against Mr. Jefferson's vest, he could hear the milkman's watch ticking, and the soothing sound had put him to sleep.

Mrs. Parker laughed as she lifted him in her arms. "He's worn out with the trip yesterday and all the excitement today," she said. "I'll put him to bed and he'll sleep all afternoon. But *where* am I going to put him? He can't sleep in the car, for we have to work in there."

"Put him in the milk wagon," said Mr. Jefferson. "I'll put up the tail gate so he can't fall out, and he'll be fine."

Pa hauled the mattress over to the wagon, and Sally made up Peter's bed. "Won't he be surprised when he wakes up and sees where he is?" she giggled.

As soon as Peter was bedded down, the whole family burst into activity. The boys carried all the small things out of the car, to get them out of the way. Ma and Sally washed the dishes.

"And I must say it makes me feel less like a gypsy to have some hot water and be able to wash the dishes right," said Ma, sitting up on her stool in front of the shelf Mr. Jefferson had made her.

Pa and Mr. Jefferson were busy unscrewing trolley car seats. Pa stopped his work to ask why Ma thought gypsies never washed dishes, and to add that if it made her feel so good to wash the dishes, he would never deprive her of the pleasure.

When the kitchen was clean, Ma helped remove the

seats, until there was space for the dining room table and benches to be set up in the end near the kitchen. The floor was swept and then scrubbed, and the boys were set to work washing the windows.

Just beyond the "dining room," Pa and Mr. Jefferson set up the china closet on one side, and a chest of drawers on the other. Beyond those were the beds, end to end, three on each side. These were neatly covered with bright spreads, and Sally arranged cushions on them. Mr. Jefferson's bed was a folding cot that was to be set up on the front platform and opened out at night.

"Let's not take out all the seats," said Sally. "Let's leave some at this end, for a living room, two on each side."

"That's right," Bill agreed. "Then we can push the backs around and sit facing each other when we want to play checkers."

"And if we want to read a book, we can sit with our backs to each other," said George.

"You know what I think?" said Mr. Jefferson. "I think it would be nice to have a porch on this trolley car."

"That's a wonderful idea," Ma said. "Then if it rained, the children wouldn't have to be cooped up inside. And judging from the looks of the sky, it might rain soon," she finished, peering out of a window.

"Look, Ma," said George, "you can look out of a window no matter what part of the house you're in."

"The clean ones you can," Ma retorted. "Hurry up

FLOOR PLAN OF TROLLEY

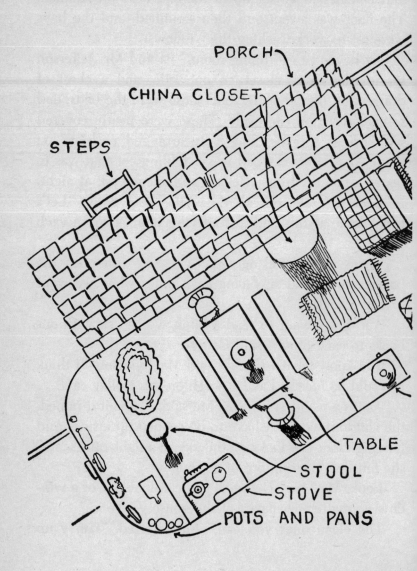

PORCH

CHINA CLOSET

STEPS

TABLE

STOOL

STOVE

POTS AND PANS

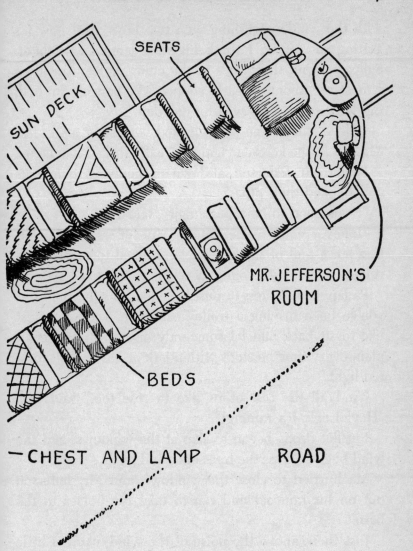

SEATS

SUN DECK

MR. JEFFERSON'S
ROOM

BEDS

CHEST AND LAMP   ROAD

with the window-washing, you two boys. And now it's getting so cloudy, I think I'll fill a lamp and light it. Sally, you put the dishes in the china closet. And then I must see about an early supper. We haven't finished, but we've done very well for one day."

Indeed, the whole place looked very snug, and after Ma had lit the kerosene lamps it really looked like home.

Pa and Mr. Jefferson sat down on the living room seats and smoked their pipes.

"Feels good to be a passenger," said Pa.

"I never could understand," Mr. Jefferson said, letting out a puff of smoke, "why you liked to go for a car ride on Sunday, the one day when you didn't have to."

Pa laughed. "Guess it must have looked silly. But after you've been driving a trolley car for a week, you just like to sit back and let somebody else do it, and complain every time he stops with a jerk or has to wait for a red light."

"And all the rest of us like to ride too," said Bill. "Hey! Look, it's raining!"

Big flat drops began to slap at the windows, and the wind began to toss the trees back and forth.

Ma hurried to close the windows, and Mr. Jefferson put on his raincoat and ran to take the horses to the barn.

Just then, above the noise of the wind, came a little wail: "Ma-ma!" It was Peter in the wagon.

"My goodness, I forgot the baby," said Ma. She didn't stop for a raincoat, but ran right out into the rain.

There was Peter standing in the back of the wagon, yelling. Ma grabbed him over the tail gate and ran back to the car.

"You're some mother," Pa teased, "forgetting your baby."

Peter cried, and the other children made funny noises to comfort him, and Ma blamed herself. And then Peter, finding he got a lot of attention, began to laugh instead of cry. They were all making so much noise that they didn't notice for some minutes that someone was knocking at the door.

Suddenly Pa jumped up and said, "I guess we have company." He put his foot on the pedal and opened the door.

"Have you room for a few more passengers?" a voice asked.

"Yes, ma'am," said Pa. "I didn't realize you were there, but come in, and welcome. We're just a little mixed up because of leaving the baby in the rain."

"Now, Pa," said Ma, "I don't know why you have to go and tell that."

The owner of the voice climbed the steps. It seemed to be a tall lady in a dripping wet rain hat and coat. Behind her came two small persons, also dripping.

"Why, it's Tom and Martha and their Aunt Hannah," said Sally.

"Hi!" Bill yelled. "I didn't recognize you at first."

The lady laughed. "Well, that's who we are—your neighbors from across the road."

Ma filled the lamps and lit them.

"Well, we certainly are glad to see you," said Ma, "and if we hadn't been so upset with forgetting the baby I might have noticed sooner that somebody was knocking at the door. If I ever move back to civilization I won't know how to behave."

"Now, Mary," said Pa, "if you would only get the idea out of your head that we're in a foreign country, you wouldn't be so mixed up."

"Now, Mr. Parker," said Ma, "here these people stand, dripping wet, and you choose this moment to tell me what kind of country we live in." And she began to bustle, helping the guests take off their raincoats, and finding places for them to sit.

Aunt Hannah held out a basket. "I know this is no time to visit you," she said, "when you've just moved not only your furniture, but your house as well. But we were so curious to see our new neighbors, that we just had to come. So I've brought a little something, for you must be so tired that you don't want to do much cooking."

Ma took the basket and said, "I knew when Sally and Bill came home with the milk and that beautiful pie, that there must be good neighbors hereabouts. And we thank you for this lovely basket, though you shouldn't have bothered, for we brought along plenty of provisions. And I do hope I can do something for you one of these days."

After this long speech, Ma heaved a sigh, and smiled, and Aunt Hannah smiled back at her, and everybody felt very pleased, because they could see that Ma and Aunt Hannah liked each other.

Now Martha, who had been hiding behind her aunt, smiled and whispered to Sally, "I brought my doll."

"Oh, let me see it," said Sally. "Come and sit on my bed and I'll show you mine." She pulled her box out from under the bed and got out her doll and all its clothes. Sally didn't really play with dolls any more, but she still liked to make clothes for them, and the two girls had a good time trying all the clothes in the box on their dolls.

George and Bill, meanwhile, had to take Tom on a tour of the car. They started at the kitchen end and worked their way to the front, where they showed him how to open and shut the door by pushing one pedal, and how to clang the bell by pushing the other.

"Boy, this is a good house," said Tom. "I'd like to live in a place like this."

"Say, you've got a real farm," said Bill, "with cows and everything. That's a lot better." He had a lot of respect for Tom's importance on the farm.

"What do you want to do when you grow up?" Tom asked.

Bill shook his head. "I always wanted to be a baseball player," he said. "But now I don't know."

"I want to be an inventor," said George. "Or maybe an explorer or a discoverer."

"You're one already!" said Bill. "What do you want to be, Tom?"

Tom clanged the bell a couple of times. "I dunno," he said. "Guess I'll be a farmer. Though I'd like real well to learn how to play the fiddle."

"The fiddle!"

"I played one once," said Tom. "The teacher in school lent me hers. It was real nice."

"Gosh! Could you really play it?"

"Sure," said Tom. "I like to play anything. So does my

Tom began to play "Yankee Doodle."

father. When he's home we play duets." He stuck his hand in his pocket and pulled out a mouth organ, and began to play "Yankee Doodle." He made the little mouth organ sing and vibrate like a trumpet. Pretty soon everybody in the car was singing "Yankee Doodle."

"My, that boy can play," Ma whispered to Aunt Hannah.

"I wish I could afford music lessons for him," Aunt Hannah whispered back.

"Go on," said Bill. "Play some more." But Tom had heard the whispering, and he shook his head and put the mouth organ away. He put his foot on the pedal and clanged the bell some more.

The rain kept pouring all the rest of the afternoon, while everybody in the car was happy, and busy. At last Pa lit the lamp on the dining-room table, and they had supper out of Aunt Hannah's picnic basket. There were fried chicken and potato salad, and rolls, and jam, and pickles, and custard pie for dessert.

It was a big basket, and there was a lot in it, and everybody ate a great deal, especially Mr. Jefferson. However, the more he ate, the less cheerful he looked. The expression on his face began to be almost as glum and cross as when he was driving his milk wagon home at eight o'clock in the morning.

"What's the matter?" Sally whispered to him.

"Nothing," Mr. Jefferson mumbled. "Just reminding myself this is only a vacation. Won't last. Just a week. Then back to cooking my own meals."

"Mr. Jefferson," said Ma, "I thought we weren't going to talk about that."

"He needs some cake," said Pa. "Nothing like cake to cheer a man up."

"Thanks," said Mr. Jefferson. He stared at the creamy wedge of custard pie in front of him. "I like pie too."

Aunt Hannah smiled and looked pleased at that, since it was her pie. "Why, thank you, Mr. Jefferson," she said. "I'm glad you like the pie. I'll make some more tomorrow. And now we have to go home. Come, children. It's past milking time."

The Parker children objected to their friends' leaving so early, but when Aunt Hannah stood up, Tom and Martha got up too. They knew that cows can't wait.

Then Mr. Jefferson surprised them. He stood up and said, "I'll go with you. I can help with the milking."

They were all amazed. "Mr. Jefferson! Do you know how to milk? When did you learn?"

"Used to work on a dairy farm," said Mr. Jefferson, gruffly. "Always been in the milk business, one way or another."

"I'd be glad to have you come," Aunt Hannah said. "We can always use some help with the milking, can't we, Tom?"

"Sure can," said Tom, "till I get big enough to lift those milk cans by myself."

When the Parkers were left by themselves, Ma exclaimed, "Well, imagine Mr. Jefferson milking a cow! I never knew he'd worked on a farm. I must ask him about that. I thought he'd always driven a milk wagon."

"Even when he was a little boy?" said George, with a very innocent look on his face.

"Georgie!" said Ma. "That will do!"

"If I were you," said Pa, "I wouldn't ask him too many questions. I'd wait and let him talk when he feels like it."

"Your father's right," said Ma. "Just let him alone, children, and let him get a good night's sleep and three meals a day and he'll be a changed man."

10. CHERRY PICKING

WHEN THE children woke up the next morning, Pa and Mr. Jefferson were sitting at the table, eating breakfast. Pa held his fork in his left hand, and with his right, he was making a list as he ate. Ma, still in her wrapper, was walking from the stove to the table and back, pouring coffee, dishing out eggs, and talking. Pa and Mr. Jefferson were going to town, and Ma was telling them what to buy.

"Yeast," she said. Pa wrote it down.

"Carrots," said Ma. "And oatmeal. And butter."

"Nails," said Mr. Jefferson. "Chicken wire."

Bill lifted his head from his pillow. "Pa," he mumbled sleepily, "don't forget the seeds."

"All right," said Pa, writing it down.

"Seeds!" Ma exclaimed. "What do you want seeds for?"

"Oh, we thought we'd plant some vegetables," said Pa, in an offhand way.

"But isn't it too late to plant anything?" Ma asked.

"We just want to see what will grow," said Pa. "Seeds don't cost much."

"Better *buy* vegetables and spend your time looking for a job," said Ma.

"Oh, the boys will take care of the garden," Pa said. "And we need a chain for the plow."

"Plow!" Ma exploded. "You going to farm?"

"Can't plant the seeds without digging up the ground," Pa explained. "And it's a lot easier to do it with horses and a plow than with a shovel."

"Well, I need a big tin washtub," said Ma.

"What's that for?" Pa asked. "You going to take in washing?"

"No," she retorted. "We have enough right here. And whatever you do, don't forget the yeast, or you'll have no bread to eat."

Mr. Jefferson drank his coffee and went out to hitch Whitey to the wagon.

Pa put the list in his pocket, took the package of lunch Ma had fixed for them, and went out. He and Mr. Jefferson climbed into the milk wagon.

"Giddap!" said Mr. Jefferson. Whitey wiggled his ears and started off.

"I wish I could have gone too," said Bill.

"Your father has a lot of business to attend to," said his mother. "You can go some other time. He has to see about getting a job, you know. Now come on, get dressed. We have work to do."

"What do we have to do?" Sally asked.

"Pick cherries," said Ma. "Aren't there more on those trees?"

"Oh, thousands," said Bill. "You want us to pick them?"

"Yes, I do," said Ma. "I wasn't planning to start on anything big, like canning, but it's not right to let good fruit spoil. I asked Pa to bring home some sugar. Now if you boys will pick the cherries—" her voice trailed away in surprise.

"What's the matter, Ma?" Sally asked.

"Why, I haven't any jars," said her mother. "They're all at home in Mr. Jefferson's barn!"

"Well, we have to pick the cherries anyway," said Bill. "The birds were eating them yesterday."

"That's true," Ma agreed. "And what we can't use, Miss Perkins might like to have."

"Let's all go," said Sally, "and have a picnic."

"Let's get Tom and Martha," said George.

Ma thought that was a good idea, and after breakfast George started across the road. Bill went with him, to carry the pail for the morning milk, and also to see that George didn't forget to return.

"And don't *you* forget to come back, either," Ma called to Bill. "Sally and I will clean up while you're gone."

Tom was just letting the cows out of the barnyard into the pasture when George and Bill arrived. He called out to them and unfastened the gate to let them in. There were two big calves in the barnyard, which stared at the visitors with their big brown eyes, and then galloped clumsily off into a corner.

"How old are they?" Bill asked.

"Oh, they're six months old," said Tom, in an indifferent tone. "Come on, I'll show you *my* calf." He led the way into the barn.

It was cool and dim inside, and smelt of hay and milk. In a big stall in a corner was a black and white cow, with a very new-looking black and white calf. The calf stood close to its mother, who was licking it. The mother

cow stopped licking and stared at Bill and George. Then the calf turned its baby face and stared at them too.

"That's a *young* calf, isn't it?" said Bill.

"Yep. Just born three days ago," said Tom.

"Gosh!" said Bill. He reached over the top of the stall and patted the baby calf's warm, silky neck.

"Isn't she a beauty?" Tom boasted. "I'm gonna raise her myself. Aunt Hannah gave her to me for my own."

Bill was full of admiration for the calf and for the whole farm. "I wish we had a farm like this," he said.

Tom shook his head. "It's not as good as it could be. We ought to have more help. We get a man to help us with the heavy work, but it takes a man on a farm all the time to make it really good. We could have a dozen cows and lots more crops." He sighed in a very grown-up way. "Aunt Hannah's in the milk room. Want to see her?"

The boys walked into a little room where Aunt Hannah was pouring milk through a strainer into some big cans.

"Good morning, neighbors," said Aunt Hannah. "It certainly is nice to have neighbors across the road. You came just in time to get your milk."

She filled Bill's pail, and then filled a pan which she set on the ground outside the door. A gray cat and three gray kittens appeared and began to lap up the milk.

Four pink tongues worked busily. Four tails stuck up in the air. Three of the tails were beautiful straight tails. But the littlest kitten had a kink in his tail, right at the end. George squatted down to examine this strange thing.

"Would you like a kitten?" Aunt Hannah asked. "Martha promised one to Sally, but you can take one now, if you like, and if your mother will let you have two cats, Sally may pick another."

"I'd like to have this one," said George, patting the one with the kinky tail. "It's a long time since we had a cat. Our black cat ran away, and took all her kittens with her." He picked up the kitten and held it close to his ear so he could hear it purr. "What happened to her tail?"

"I think she got in a cow's stall," said Tom, "and the cow must have stepped on her tail. She's always getting into something."

Bill laughed. "Just like George. You picked the right one, Georgie."

Then he remembered what he had come for. "Ma wants to know if you would all like to go on a picnic with us," he said. "We want to pick cherries up on the hill back of our barn, and take a picnic lunch."

"That's a splendid idea," said Aunt Hannah. "Mr. Jefferson helped with the milking again today, so we're way ahead with our work."

"Mr. Jefferson came over this morning!" Bill said. "We never knew it. We must have been asleep. Gosh! I wish I could milk. Then I'd come and help you too."

"Come over yourself," Aunt Hannah said. "We'll teach you."

Tom laughed. "Pretty soon Aunt Hannah and I won't

have to do a thing. We'll sit on the porch and give orders."

"That's right," said Aunt Hannah. "Now, if Sally will come and help Martha with the housework, there won't be anything left for me to do."

"You'll still have to do the cooking, Aunt Hannah," said Tom. "I wouldn't eat Martha's cooking."

"Hm! Sally's either," said Bill. "All she can make is fudge."

"Well, anyway," said Aunt Hannah, "Martha is making the beds and washing the dishes today, and as soon as we're all done, we'll be over."

Bill and George went back more slowly than they had come, since Bill had the milk to carry, and George had the kitten with the kinky tail.

When Ma saw the kitten she said, "Hm! Seems as if our family just keeps on growing. First two chickens, and then a cat. What next?"

"Aunt Hannah said we could have another cat," said George. "One for Sally."

"No indeed," said Ma. "One is plenty. Here's a saucer for it, and you have to feed it yourself, mind. Don't expect me to remember it. I have enough to do."

"I'll help you remember, Georgie," said Sally. "I think it's a darling. Let's call it Kinky."

At this moment Peter spied the kitten, and with a joyful cry of "Kittee!" he ran as fast as he could to hug the little cat in his arms. But the kitten was old enough to take care of itself. Like a streak of lightning it galloped the length of the beds and leaped lightly upon the top of the china closet. There it sat, looking down at the Parkers.

"We won't have to worry about Peter hurting this cat," said Sally. "But we'd better close all the windows, or she'll run away while we're out."

In a little while Aunt Hannah and Tom and Martha arrived, with pails for the cherries and their basket of lunch. The Parkers gathered up all the pails and saucepans they could find. Bill carried an old blanket for Peter to take his nap on, and they all started for the barn, where they left their lunches to be out of the sun. Then they went on to the orchard.

"My goodness!" said Aunt Hannah, when she saw the red cherries. "I never knew there were so many."

"There weren't last year," said Tom. "I was over here but there were only a few, and the birds got most of them."

"It's lucky you came," said Aunt Hannah to Ma, "or the birds would have had these too, and they've had them long enough now."

"How long?" Ma asked.

"Well, the old man who owned this place moved away about five years ago," said Aunt Hannah, "and then the house burned down—"

"Where was the house?" George asked.

Tom pointed up the hill. "Up there back of the barn," he said. "There isn't anything there now except some bricks and a lot of stickers and poison ivy."

Bill was getting restless. He rattled his pail and said, "Uh—Ma—"

"Bill thinks we ought to be getting busy," said Ma. "All right, boys, you climb the trees and start picking."

Each boy climbed a tree. As they filled their little pails, they handed them down to Mrs. Parker or Aunt Hannah, who emptied the cherries into a milk pail. The two ladies were so busy talking and getting acquainted, that they often had to be called several times before they heard the boys.

Sally and Martha were likewise getting better acquainted as they took care of little Peter, who wanted to eat all the rotten cherries or green apples he could find on the ground.

Sally said, "I was so glad when I saw there was a girl here. It's not that I don't like the boys, but I do like to see a girl once in a while. I wish we'd have another baby, and maybe it would be a girl. But then," she went on thoughtfully, "it wouldn't be anywhere near my age, of course."

"Well, I'm glad you have Peter," said Martha. "Of course he isn't really a baby any more, but still he's nice to play with." She tickled the back of Peter's neck, and he turned around and grinned at her, and offered her a green apple which he had just found.

"Do you live here all the time?" Sally asked.

"Yes," said Martha. "Mama died when I was a little tiny baby. And Papa travels around on boats. He's an engineer. So he can't take us along, and we stay with Aunt Hannah."

At last they heard Ma's voice calling, "All right, boys, we've got all we can take now. You'd better come down and we'll have lunch."

11. GEORGE MAKES ANOTHER DISCOVERY

THE BOYS scrambled down out of the trees. Their mouths and hands were stained red from the cherries, and they were hot and dirty.

"You boys go over to the spring and wash your faces," said Ma.

"I wish we could swim in it," said George.

"Well, you found it," Bill said. "Why didn't you find a lake instead of a spring, while you were at it?"

"You can't find what isn't there," George retorted. "And some people can't even find what *is* there."

Ma called after them, "Bring the milk back with you when you come." Then she explained to Aunt Hannah: "We keep the milk in the spring. It's as cold as an icebox."

"Mama," Sally asked, "what were you going to use for an icebox if there hadn't been any spring?"

Her mother looked at her. She seemed puzzled. She stopped taking sandwiches out of the picnic basket and sat back on her heels. Then she laughed and said, "To tell the truth, if I didn't forget all about that! I don't know what I *was* planning to use. And me with a baby! That shows how we get used to civilization."

"You could have used our icebox," said Aunt Hannah.

"Well, that would have been very nice of you," said Ma, "but of course we didn't know you'd be here either. But we certainly are glad you are."

After lunch everybody lay down on the grass for a rest. It was so warm and quiet under the trees, that before long Ma and Aunt Hannah really fell asleep. So did Peter, stretched out on his blanket. Bill and Tom talked quietly together under one tree, and Sally and Martha under another.

George lay on his back, staring up at the branches over his head. He looked over at Bill and Tom. Then at Sally and Martha. Then at Peter. He wished he had a blanket like Peter's to lie on. The grass tickled his neck and his arms and legs, and it even tickled right through his shirt. And he was thirsty. He wished he had a drink. He got up and wandered in the direction of the spring.

Bill looked up at him.

"I'm going to get a drink," said George as he passed.

"Well, don't drink up the whole spring," said Bill.

"Maybe I will, maybe I won't," George retorted.

The spring water was cold and good. George lay on his stomach and cupped his hands in the water. He drank and drank until he felt all cool inside. He splashed the water on his face. His arms felt nice and cool too, and most of the dirt was washed off them. He thought it would be nice to put his feet in.

Then he thought, "I guess you shouldn't put your feet in a spring that everybody drinks out of."

Then he thought, "But I put my hands in, and they were just as dirty as my feet. But I guess it's all right. The water runs away and the dirt will get washed out. Anyhow it's clean dirt."

He was about to put his feet in, when he thought, "I wonder where it *does* run to."

He got up and looked. The water trickled off through the grass. It had worn a little path for itself through the field. He could see where the grass was taller along its course. It wandered along until it got to the orchard and then it disappeared among the trees.

George walked all around the spring. The tall grass was trampled around it, where they had been stepping on it the last two days. Pa had put a big pot into the spring, and Ma kept her milk can and her butter there.

Suddenly George noticed something. Another little path led away from the spring on the other side. It led up the hill. It was a very faint path, scarcely more than the mark a stick would make if you dragged it over the grass.

"I wonder who made that path," George said. "It's pretty old. Nobody's been here for years." He walked in the path, up the side of the hill behind the barn.

The ground was covered with scrubby bushes and

blackberry vines. The vines caught at his legs and scratched him, and it was hot in the sun. There were a few scraggly trees with poison ivy climbing up them.

Something was sticking up out of the bushes and blackberry vines. He walked over to it. It was the remains of a chimney.

"Jumping Jupiter!" he whispered to himself.

This was where the house had been—the farmhouse that burned down. Some bricks from the top of the chimney lay on the ground. Weeds grew out of the remains of the fireplace. There was a heap of rusty iron that had once been a kitchen stove, and there were some bits of charred wood. That was all.

The house had burned down, and the grass and bushes had covered up the place, so you could hardly see where it had been. George looked around for the path he had been following. The path had stopped. This was as far as it went.

"Jumping Jupiter!" said George again. "That was their path to the spring. They walked down there to get their water. I wonder why they didn't build the house down near the spring. They wouldn't have had to carry the water so far. Well, maybe they wanted the house up where they could get a good view of everything." He looked down at the barn, and farther down at the trolley car sitting on the tracks beside the road.

"I guess," he said, "every time they wanted a pail of water they'd send one of the boys. They'd say, 'Hey, George, go get a pail of water.' That's how people are."

Suddenly he heard voices. "George! George! Where are you? Come back here! Oh, George!"

"All right, I'm coming," he shouted, and turned and ran back down the hill. He was glad to get away from that lonesome place. As he passed the spring, he met the rest of the party heading for the lane, carrying their baskets and pails full of cherries.

"Georgie!" his mother exclaimed. "Where in heaven's name have you been? We called and called. We thought you were lost."

"No, Ma, I wasn't lost. I just went for a walk," said George.

"Well, we woke up and you were nowhere in sight. Here, carry the blanket. And don't trail it on the ground."

George took the blanket, and they proceeded slowly toward the trolley car. It gleamed bright yellow in the afternoon sun. An automobile passing on the road slowed down and then speeded up again. Then another car did the same thing.

"Well, what do you think of that!" said Ma. "The cars slow down when they go past our trolley. I wonder why. I didn't notice that yesterday. But then I was so busy I suppose I didn't notice much of anything."

"I know why they do it," said Sally. "The trolley car looks so funny to them."

"That's so," said her mother. "It certainly must look funny. I suppose if I were going past in a car and saw that thing standing in the middle of the scenery, with

two hens tied to its wheels, I'd about laugh my head
off."

Now around the bend in the road came a horse-drawn
wagon.

"There come Pa and Mr. Jefferson!" Bill shouted.
"Come on, let's run!" and he broke into a gallop.

The others hurried as well as they could, with all the
things they had to carry, but the milk wagon got there
first. Pa and Mr. Jefferson were climbing down when
the children arrived.

"What did you get?" they asked. "Did you get the
seeds? The chicken feed? Anything for me?"

"Here, here," said Pa, looking very cheerful. "We
got a lot of things. Hold your horses!" He went around
to the back of the wagon.

"Did you get a job?" Ma asked.

"No," said Pa, "but see here." And he lifted down a
crate.

Ten hens and a rooster stuck their heads out between
the slats and squawked angrily.

"Aren't they fine?" Pa asked, proudly. "They're Rhode
Island Reds."

"They sure are," said Bill, hoisting one end of the
crate. "Gosh, they're swell!" He and his father looked
at each other and grinned. "Come on, let's take them up
to the barn. I'll get water for them."

But Ma wasn't so pleased.

"What in the name of all that's good and beautiful
are you going to do with those?" she inquired.

The milk wagon got there first.

"Feed and water 'em, like Bill says," said Pa. "And what about us? Did you make a cake? Is our supper ready?"

"Why, no," said Ma, "we were busy saving the cherries."

"Supper!" Peter wailed.

And at that sound, Ma turned and walked up the steps into the car. After all, this was no time to stand and ask questions.

"Come, Tom and Martha," said Aunt Hannah. "Say good-by. We'll see our friends tomorrow."

"I'll be over for the milking," Mr. Jefferson called.

"And so will I," Bill shouted.

12.   PA IS THE BOSS

WHILE MA was busy getting supper, and putting Peter to bed, she appeared calm and cheerful. But after the dishes were done and they were all sitting around the table, Ma frowned over her mending.

Mr. Jefferson was whittling a peg for his milk wagon. Pa was sorting nails. The boys were playing Chinese checkers. Everybody was busy but Sally, who sat with Kinky in her lap, stroking the soft fur and looking from one to the other of the family.

She was surprised when she saw Ma's frown.

"What's the matter, Ma?" she asked.

"Oh, nothing," said Ma, biting off her thread, and rummaging in the basket for the mending cotton.

Bill gave his mother a sharp look. Then he jumped his blue marble over four of George's red ones, and said, "Ma doesn't like those chickens Pa bought."

"Whaff wrong wiv vuh shickensh?" Pa asked. He had

Pa was sorting nails.

several nails in his mouth, so he couldn't speak very clearly.

"Take those nails out of your mouth, Mr. Parker," said Ma, "before you swallow them and we have more trouble."

Pa spat out the nails, and repeated. "What's the matter with the chickens?"

"Well," said Ma, "you didn't say you were going to get a lot of livestock. I was just wondering what we would feed them, to say nothing of what we're going to feed the children. And while I think it would be wrong not to take care of the trees up yonder, which are there already, I don't think we can afford to take up farming, which I always heard even farmers couldn't make a living at."

"Now, Mary," said Pa, "it's true I haven't had a chance to do much explaining, but those chickens were a bargain. I didn't pay but five dollars for the lot. I bought them from the man at the lumber yard, where we got the nails and cement—"

"Cement!" Ma exclaimed. "What in the world is that for?"

"Why, to fix the barn floor, so the cow won't put her foot in a hole and break a leg."

"Cow!" Ma was simply flabbergasted. The children looked from one parent to the other, wondering what would happen next.

"Are we getting a cow?" Bill asked. "That's swell!"

Pa looked at Mr. Jefferson. "You speak up," he said, and began to sort nails again.

Mr. Jefferson took his pipe out of his mouth. "It's really my cow," he said. "Thought it was a shame for all this pasture land to go to waste. Barn's empty too. So I thought I'd buy a cow and keep it here."

"But, Mr. Jefferson," said Sally, "what will we do with all the milk?"

"I thought of that," said Mr. Jefferson. "You use as much as you can. Milk, butter, cheese. Then sell the rest to the cheese factory, same as Miss Perkins does. Man stops for her milk with the truck, he can take ours too."

"But what about when we go away from here," said Ma. "How long do you folks consider that we are going to stay in this place, nice as it is?"

"Well, Mary," said Pa, "it's this way. We've only been here a few days. But you know I was brought up in the country. And somehow it's all come back to me, and I'm getting to like this place more and more. I thought I'd spend a few days fixing it up, so's we can live here comfortably. We still have a little money. I'm sure I can get a job when it's necessary. And when we go, we can always sell anything that we don't want. But as long as we're here, we might as well have eggs and milk—"

"And butter and cheese," Sally interrupted. "We could make those. Do you know how, Ma?"

"If I don't I can learn," said Ma. "If we're going to

have a cow, we might as well make use of the milk. Now, Mr. Jefferson," she went on, turning to him, "you've been a good friend to us, and of course we'll be glad to take care of your cow, though we ought to pay for the milk we use. But I surely would like it if you could stay with us as a member of the family. I have a feeling you'd like to take care of that cow yourself."

Here Bill interrupted. "Why don't you stay, Mr. Jefferson? It's nice here. We want you to stay."

Mr. Jefferson shook his head sadly. He looked so gloomy that Sally was almost afraid he was going to cry, except that she had never seen a grown-up cry.

"Got to get back to my job," he muttered, pulling out his handkerchief and blowing his nose. Then he looked up and scowled terribly. He glared at one member of the family after another, till they were all frightened. They couldn't imagine what he might do. Then he exploded.

"I won't do it!" he said. "I'll stay another week! Got a right to two weeks' vacation in ten years!"

"I'm very glad you can do that, Mr. Jefferson," Ma said. "Will you have to write and ask the company to let you take another week?"

Mr. Jefferson got red in the face. He fidgeted in his chair. Then he said, in an embarrassed voice, "No, I won't. I asked for two weeks in the beginning. But I wasn't sure I'd take two. Just said I'd take one, till I saw how I liked it. *And I like it,*" he finished up in a defiant tone.

"That's fine," said Ma. "And now I have something more to say. I was worried this afternoon, Mr. Parker, when you came home without a job, but with eleven chickens. But now I've decided not to be worried. You've always provided for this family, and I expect you'll go on providing, and if you don't, it won't be because you don't want to. So from now on I won't say another word, but let you be the boss of this family. When you decide to move on, we'll move on. And if you decide to buy a herd of goats, or any other creatures, I won't say a word. And if we run out of money, why, I'll bake bread and sell it if I have to. And that's all. Children, is that all right with you?"

"Oh, yes," said all three children. And Bill added, "It's swell."

Sally had a suggestion. "We could put the bread out in front in the china closet, with a big sign, For Sale."

Ma didn't look so pleased with that suggestion, but before she could say anything, Pa spoke up, with three or four nails in his mouth: "Your mother said I was the boss, and so I begin by saying that it's time you children went to bed, for we have lots of work to do tomorrow."

"I told you before," said Ma, "to take those nails out of your mouth before you swallow them."

"Well, Mary," said Mr. Parker, laughing, "I thought you said I was the boss, but I see you are going to be the boss of what does or doesn't go into our stomachs. All right. From now on, I don't put nails in my mouth or stomach. Now, kids, go to bed."

Sally got up, still hugging the kitten.

"Can I have the kitten?" George asked. "I want her to sleep with me." He held out his arms for the cat.

"Oh, let me have her tonight," said Sally.

"Nobody is to sleep with the kitten," said Ma. "The kitten will have her own bed. Now you decide where to put her."

This was a problem. Sally proposed the box under her bed. She pulled it out and put Kinky in among the dolls' clothes.

"There, that's a nice soft bed for you," she said. But Kinky jumped right out and leaped up on George's pillow.

The children laughed. But Pa, enjoying his role of boss, said, "Put the cat outside. Cats don't have to sleep in the house."

"Oh, no, Pa!" George cried. "She'd get lost."

"Well, your mother said she couldn't sleep with you," said Pa. "That's final."

"I know," said Bill. "That old birdcage that Georgie found. Put her in there."

"Okay," said George. He hurried to get the cage down off the nail where it had been hung, and Sally made a soft bed of rags in the bottom of the cage. They put Kinky in, and she curled herself up into a ball and went to sleep.

"Now, George," Pa went on, "you get a pail of water

before you go to bed, so we'll have it in the morning. Take the flashlight."

"Okay, Pa," said George, "but I have an idea."

"George," said his mother, "Pa said you should go for water. Hurry up. Here's the pail."

"Yes, Ma," said George. "But I want to tell Pa my swell idea before I forget about it. It just came into my mind."

Bill gave his younger brother a black look and said, "I bet it has something to do with not getting the water."

George glared at Bill, and said, "Yep, that's right. I was thinking, why don't we run a pipe from the spring to here, and then the water will come down by itself. Then we won't have to go up after it."

Pa stared at his son. Then he slapped his hand down on the table and all the nails jumped.

"By gum!" he exclaimed. "That's a smart idea! How'd you think of that, son?"

"Oh, it just came in my mind," said George, modestly. "I was looking around up by the spring and I thought of it."

"And you were afraid you'd forget it!" said Bill, with scorn.

"Yes," said George. "And you could pipe it to the barn too, maybe." And he picked up the pail and went for the water.

Pa and Bill and Mr. Jefferson exchanged grins.

"That's a good idea, Pa," said Bill. He was really proud of his kid brother, though he did like to tease him.

Pa nodded. "The boy's got a good head on him. But don't tell him I said so. It'll make him conceited."

"I heard you, Pa," George called from outside.

"Fresh kid," Bill muttered.

13. FARMING IS FUN

WHEN BILL opened his eyes, Mr. Jefferson was stirring about, behind the curtain that separated the front platform from the rest of the car. The rest of the family was still asleep.

"I'd better hurry," Bill whispered to himself. He sat up in bed. He had a strong temptation to lie down again and take another snooze in his nice soft pillow. But he fought the weakness and it went away. Very quietly he stood up and put on his overalls and shirt. He took his shoes in his hand and tiptoed out to the platform. Mr. Jefferson was just tying his boots.

"I'm going to help you milk," said Bill.

Mr. Jefferson nodded. They went out and across the road. The morning was gray. A mist hung over the fields, and there was a cool damp smell in the air.

"Think it's going to rain?" Bill asked.

Mr. Jefferson pointed to the horizon, where the sun made a bright spot in the mist.

"Won't rain when you can see the sun like that," said

Mr. Jefferson. "Sun'll burn off the mist when it gets high. It'll be a hot day."

Rex came bounding down the lane to meet them, barking and whistling through his nose. He flattened his ears down and wiggled his hind quarters and wagged his tail all together. Bill patted his head, but didn't stop to play. There was work to do this morning. They proceeded to the barn.

Tom was in there, measuring mash into the troughs in front of the cows.

Mr. Jefferson and Tom each took a pail and a little stool and sat down beside a cow and started to milk. Bill stood and watched Mr. Jefferson. He had had his first lesson the night before, but he wanted to watch a little. It was quiet in the barn. The only sounds were the swishing of the cows' tails, as they stood munching their mash, and the drumming sound of the milk in the pails. Bill liked it. He liked the smell, and he liked the quiet, peaceful feeling.

He got a pail and a stool too and sat down beside the brown cow he had milked the night before. He grabbed one teat in each hand, and pulled, with the special kind of pull that Tom had showed him. Two streams of milk drummed down into the pail. He did it again and again. He did it slowly. When Tom and Mr. Jefferson were all through, Tom came over to see how Bill was getting along. The pail was nearly full.

"You're good," said Tom.

Two streams of milk drummed down into the pail.

"Not as good as you," said Bill.

"Well, you just started yesterday," Tom answered. "I've been doing it since I was seven. Let me in there. I'll just strip her."

Tom sat down on the stool and squeezed the last drops of milk out of the cow's udder. Bill stretched his arms and legs.

"Oh, boy!" he said. "It's fun. I like it."

"You learned fast," said Tom. "You practice a little more and you'll get more speed." And he went to pour the milk into the big can.

On the way home, Bill and Mr. Jefferson talked about the cow they were going to get.

"I'll take care of her for you, Mr. Jefferson," Bill said.

Mr. Jefferson nodded. "Glad to have you do it," he said. "Just remember, you've got to milk her night and morning, always the same time. And always give her the same amount of mash. Got to be regular. That's the thing, when you're taking care of animals."

When they got home to the trolley car, Ma was stirring the oatmeal, and Sally was busy setting the breakfast table.

"Breakfast ready?" Bill demanded. "I'm starved." He handed Ma the bucket of milk and went to wash up. "Come on, Sally, make it snappy."

"You act like a regular farm hand," said Pa.

"He'll make a good dairy man," Mr. Jefferson said. "Milked a cow himself, all but the stripping."

Bill felt his face getting red. He felt very proud. He didn't know Mr. Jefferson had noticed.

"By the way, Bill," said Pa, as they sat down, "we haven't played any baseball yet."

Bill stopped shoveling oatmeal into his mouth and looked up. "You know we haven't got time for baseball," he said. "We have to start the plowing."

"They think plowing is so important," said Sally, with a sniff. "Come on, Ma. We can't sit here all day. We have to start the bread."

"Oh, is that so!" said Bill. "Where do you think you'd *get* bread if nobody did any plowing or planting?" And he seized a slice of bread, spread it thickly with butter and then with jam, and devoured half of it in one bite.

Right after breakfast the menfolk started for the barn. Pa carried the sack of chicken feed, Bill had a pail of nails, George lugged the chain for the plow and Mr. Jefferson had a bag of cement. Sally and her mother watched them go. Then they smiled at each other and started cleaning house.

Up at the barn, Pa dragged out the old plow. It was covered with rust, but it was still sound. Mr. Jefferson helped him rig up a harness for the horses. Whitey, in his sun hat, was a surprised-looking horse. He kept turning around to see what was being fastened on behind him. This made the boys laugh. Whitey hung his head and crossed one hoof in front of the other.

"His feelings are hurt," said Mr. Jefferson.

Whitey was a surprised-looking horse.

"How do you know?" Bill asked.

"I can tell," said Mr. Jefferson. "He doesn't like to be laughed at. And besides, he's never been hitched to a plow and he can't figure it out."

The other horse didn't seem to care what he was hitched to.

"He has no imagination," said Mr. Jefferson.

"You mean he's stupid?" Bill asked.

"You don't have to say it right in front of him," said Mr. Jefferson. "He has feelings."

"Now," said Pa, when the horses were hitched, "if you two experts think the horses' feelings won't be too

much hurt, we'll ask them to please get started and plow
a strip thirty feet long."

"Giddap!" said Bill.

"You forgot to say please," said Pa.

He and Bill set out on their first furrow. It was hard
going. The grass was tough. The two horses had to strain
hard to pull the rusty blade through the packed earth.
And it was a long time since Mr. Parker had guided a
plow. His shirt was wet with perspiration by the time
they had gone the allotted thirty feet.

"This is harder than steering a street car," said he.

"But it's more fun, isn't it, Pa?" Bill asked, grinning
at him.

"Sure is, son," said Pa. "Giddap!"

Mr. Jefferson, meanwhile, had let the chickens out in
the grass. They squawked happily at being released,
and ran here and there, clucking to each other, and
pecking for bugs and seeds.

"Won't they run away, Mr. Jefferson?" George asked.

"They'll come back mighty quick when I throw 'em
some corn," said Mr. Jefferson. "Now I'm going to drive
in some posts and make a run for them with that
chicken wire."

George watched the hens for a while. Then he went
inside the barn. It was cool and dark in there. Wisps of
hay hung down from the loft above, and in a pile on the
floor there was a hollow place scooped out by some hen
a long time ago.

George wandered about the barn. He could see daylight through the cracks in the walls where the boards had been shrunk by the rain and sun. From outside he could hear the sound of Mr. Jefferson's hammer blows, and his father's voice calling to the horses. Everybody was working. There didn't seem to be much for him to do. He didn't care. He liked to look around, just to see what he could find.

A bird darted in through the open door and flew up to the rafters. There was a sound of tiny voices peeping. Must be a nest up there, he thought.

His eye rested on a rusty old shovel in a corner. He picked it up and poked at the pile of hay. There was a squeak-squeaking noise and a scurrying of tiny feet. A mouse nest! He got down on his knees and pushed the hay back carefully. In a little hollow he found a tiny nest, all soft with bits of dust and hair, and four squirming, wriggling little pink mice, half as long as his little finger. He covered them up with the hay again so they wouldn't get cold.

Then on a ledge he saw an old tin coffee can. He pried the cover off. It was half full of some kind of seeds.

He wondered what they were.

"Guess I'll plant those," he thought. "Surprise everybody."

He took the shovel and the can of seeds and went out behind the barn. He dug some holes and pushed the seeds in and covered them over. Then he stood up and looked across the field. He could see Pa and Bill way off there with the horses. There was quite a big patch of plowed ground, and they were unhitching the horses from the plow.

Then he heard Pa calling: "George! Oh, George! Where are you?"

"Here I am, Pa!" he shouted. He ran across the field to them. "I planted some seeds."

"Seeds!" said Pa. "Where'd you get seeds? You take the seeds I bought yesterday?"

"No, Pa," said George. "I found them in the barn."

"What kind of seeds were they?"

"I don't know," said George. "Maybe they were watermelon seeds. I hope so. I like watermelon."

"Probably won't grow," said his father. "Why, those seeds must have been there five years. They couldn't be any good."

"Well, can I water them?"

"Sure," said Pa. "Water doesn't cost anything. Get the pail, and then take a pail of water back to the house with you. I mean the car."

George ran for the pail, and caught up with Bill, who was leading Whitey to the spring for a drink.

"Look at him," said Bill, slapping Whitey's side. "He's sweating. Plowing sure is hard work."

"You like it?" George asked.

"I sure do," said Bill. "And now I *know* what I'm going to be when I grow up. Not a baseball player. I'm going to be a *farmer!*"

"You are!" said George, admiringly.

"Yep," said Bill. He rested his hand on Whitey as the

horse sloshed the water into himself. "Look at him drink! I never thought I'd be plowing a field with him!"

Pa came up with the other horse, and Whitey moved over. When the horses had had their fill, they were turned loose to graze in the field, and Pa and the boys washed their faces in the cold spring water, and took a good long drink apiece.

Just then there was a loud clattering noise from the trolley car. Sally was banging on a tin pan with a spoon. It was the dinner bell.

"Just in time," said Bill. "I would have starved to death in another minute."

When the field hands arrived at the car they found the table set and wonderful smells coming from the stove.

"I hope you have a lot of food, Ma," said Bill. "We're awfully hungry."

"What, again?" Ma exclaimed, ladling out beef stew. "I hope you planted a lot of stuff this morning. I can't keep up with farmers' appetites."

"Bill plowed," said George. "He's gonna be a farmer when he grows up."

"Well, I can't wait till he grows up," said Ma. "The way you're all eating, I'll need some extra crops in about a week."

"That ground is awful hard, Ma," said Bill, with his mouth full of stew. "I need lots of strength to plow it." And he held out his plate for more.

"What do you think we've been doing while you were gone?" said Sally.

"Making bread," said Bill, sniffing in the direction of a large bowl covered with a clean towel.

"That's not all," said Sally. "Churning!"

"Churning!"

"Aunt Hannah and Martha came over," Sally went on, "and brought their churn, and a pail of cream. It's an awful old churn, but it worked fine. Look!" And she held up the butter plate.

"Golly!" said George. "I thought you had to go to the store for that!"

"Silly!" said his sister, in a superior way. "How do you think the old pioneers got butter? There weren't any stores!"

"Maybe they used peanut butter," said George.

"Or jam," said Bill. "Hey, Ma, are you going to make jam out of those cherries we picked yesterday?"

"I was coming to that," said Ma. "I'm going over to Miss Perkins' house tomorrow to make preserves. Miss Perkins says she has a cellar full of jars, and we're going to do the preserving over there and share the jam. We put the cherries in her cellar to keep cool, and I'm going over right after breakfast."

"May I go too?" Sally asked.

"You'd better stay here, honey," her mother said. "I don't want to take Peter—he'd only be in the way—so you stay here and mind him. Martha can come and keep you company."

"Oh," said Sally, looking disappointed.

"Making preserves isn't much fun," said Ma. "It's hot and sticky."

"But why do I always have to be the one to take care of things? Why can't Bill stay?"

"You're the oldest," said her mother. "I feel I can depend on you."

Sally pouted. "I'm tired of being the oldest," she said.

"It's a responsibility," said Ma. "But there are some good things about it too. You'll be glad of it one of these days."

14. SALLY DOES SOME BUSINESS

NEXT MORNING, after the house was cleaned up, Mrs. Parker set out for Aunt Hannah's kitchen. She had said a great deal about how hot and sticky one got when putting up preserves, but she didn't look as if she would rather not go. In fact, she seemed eager to get there. She said she wanted to get it over with.

"You can let Peter play in the big tub," she said to Sally. "And if you should need anything, or get in trouble, though I don't see why you should, just bang on that pan with the wooden spoon, and either Pa or I will come over. And here comes Martha now, to keep you company. And don't forget that soup cooking on the stove. Just stir it once in a while and turn the fire out at eleven o'clock."

"All right, Ma, I won't forget," said Sally.

Martha had brought her doll in a basket, and she sat down on the grass behind the trolley car to sew a dress for her child. Sally brought out some sewing too.

She felt very much like Martha's big sister, as she watched the brown curly head bent over the work.

"Really," she thought to herself, "I'm getting almost too big for dolls. I ought to give my doll to Martha."

Little Peter played near them, digging with an old spoon and shoveling the sandy soil into a tin can.

Up near the barn they could see Mr. Parker stooping over his tomato plants.

It was a hot, sunny day. After awhile Peter got himself covered with dust, and began to complain.

"Mother said I could let him play in the tub," said Sally. "Come on, let's get it."

She and Martha got the washtub down from its nail on the side of the car, and poured two pails of water into it. Peter was pleased. He ran to the tub and leaned over the edge.

"Want to get in," he said.

Sally took off his sunsuit and lifted him into the water, which was not cold, as it had been standing in the sun. Peter splashed with his hands and feet, and poured water from the can over his little fat stomach.

"I'd better go and stir the soup again," said Sally, sticking her needle into her work. "You watch Peter for me."

She climbed the steps to the kitchen. A car passed by in the road, slowed down, and then went on. Sally was used to it by this time, and paid no attention.

Then another car did the same thing. But this time,

instead of going on, the automobile really stopped. After a minute the driver honked his horn.

Sally put her foot on the button and opened the door, and looked out.

A nice-looking man put his head out of the car window. "Are you serving lunch yet?" he asked.

"What!" said Sally, in astonishment.

"I say, can we get some lunch?"

"Who?" said Sally.

"My little boy and I," said the man. "I know it's early for lunch, but we had our breakfast very early. About six o'clock. The poor kid is tired and hungry."

Sally was so surprised she couldn't think of an answer. She just stared at the nice-looking man and his little boy in the automobile. The little boy wasn't much bigger than Peter.

The man said, "It doesn't have to be much. Just a couple of eggs and a glass of milk."

"Wait a minute," said Sally. "I'll be right back."

She ran and called out the kitchen door to Martha. "What shall I do? There's a man out there with a little boy, and they want lunch. Shall I give them some lunch?"

"Lunch!" said Martha, looking scared. "Why do they come here for lunch?"

"Don't you see?" said Sally. "They think it's a lunch wagon. That's why all those cars have been stopping. They all thought the trolley car was a diner—you know, a place to eat in. I'll call Ma." And she was just about to run for the pan and spoon, when another idea struck her.

After all, she was the oldest, and ought to be able to think for herself. What would Ma do, if a man and a little boy came and asked for lunch? Why, feed them, of course.

She went out front and said, "All right, I can give you some lunch. You come on in, and I'll have it ready in a minute."

Now it was the man's turn to look surprised. He began: "Are you—er—I mean, is your mother—that is, isn't anybody here but you?"

Sally smiled at him. "My mother's across the road making jam, and Pa and the boys are up by the barn, but I can give you and your little boy some lunch."

The man got out of the car, and held the door open for his little boy to get down. The boy seized his father's finger and stared at Sally.

"This is Billy," said the man.

"Maybe he would like to come round to the back and play with my little brother while I'm getting lunch," said Sally. She led the way to where Peter was still splashing in his tub.

When Martha saw the strangers she looked scared.

"It's all right, Martha," said Sally. "I decided to fix lunch. The soup is just about done."

"But wait a minute," said the man. "I thought this

was a lunch wagon. You know, one of those dining cars you see along the road. I never would have bothered you otherwise. I thought it was odd you had no sign out, but I figured it was a new place and the sign wasn't ready yet."

"Well, I'm glad you stopped," said Sally. "Cars have been stopping ever since we moved out here, and we couldn't understand why. Now I've found out."

"Moved out here!" said the man. "What do you mean?"

"We live here," said Sally. "We moved out here last Saturday. If you want to sit here and mind the children, I'll go in and set the table."

"All right," said the man, laughing. "You're a smart little girl, and I leave it all to you."

Sally seized Martha's hand and pulled her along to the kitchen.

"Now you must help me," she said. "You set the table while I cook some eggs." She cut off some slices of Ma's bread, and put water on to boil for the eggs. "Now, Martha, you go up to the spring and get the butter and the boiled milk for the children."

As Martha started for the spring, Sally looked out of the window. Apparently Billy couldn't bear to watch Peter enjoying himself alone in the tub, for he had sat down and was taking off his shoes and socks.

"Let him get in," said Sally. "It'll cool him off."

So Billy's suit came off, and soon two naked little

boys were splashing in the tub. Billy's father lay back on the grass and closed his eyes. He looked tired.

"Poor man," Sally thought. "It must be hard for him to take care of that little boy. I wonder where his wife is."

When lunch was ready, Sally went out with two towels.

"Time to come out now," she said.

Billy and Peter looked at her indignantly. They wouldn't come out! They were having fun!

"No!" they shouted. They had to be lifted out, and as soon as they were out they began to run around and get dirty.

"Come and get dressed," Billy's father called.

"No!" Billy shouted, running around in the dust.

"No!" Peter screamed, getting back into the tub.

Then Sally had an idea. Peter was always ready for food. "Peter," she said, "want some bread and butter? Nice bread and butter?"

Peter stood still. Then he climbed out of the tub and started for the kitchen. Billy followed. They let themselves be dried and dressed, and soon they were sitting down to a nice lunch of soup, eggs, bread and butter, and cherries.

"This is the best place we've stopped at, isn't it, Billy?" said his father.

"More milk," said Billy, with his mouth full of bread and egg.

"That's the first time he's asked for more of anything since I can remember," said his father. "I wish I could stay right here and just let him play with Peter and eat. But we must get on. Billy's going to stay with his grandmother on her farm."

"He'll have fun on the farm, won't he?" said Sally.

"Of course he will. Now we have to get started. We have two hundred miles to go, and I want to get there by tomorrow morning."

Billy didn't want to go, and Peter looked as if he might cry, till Sally said, "Maybe Billy will come back some day and play with Peter again." That cheered them up.

As Sally put out her hand to say good-by, Billy's father took it and put something into it. Sally looked, and saw two dollar bills.

"Oh, no," she said. "Please don't give me that. Ma wouldn't like it."

She tried to give it back, but he wouldn't take it.

"Look here," he said, "we thought this was a lunch wagon, and we stopped and asked for lunch, and now we have to pay for it."

"But not two dollars!" Sally protested.

"It was worth a lot more," said he. "I didn't think I'd ever see a little girl like you running a lunch wagon, and I don't know when I've had such a good time."

And with that he dumped Billy into the car, got in himself and slammed the door and was off. The children waved after them.

Sally looked down at the two dollars in her hand. "What do you think of that?" she said. "Won't Ma be surprised!"

"I wonder where the little boy's mother is," said Martha.

"So do I," said Sally. "Well, maybe she's having another baby, and he's going to stay with his grandmother in the country for the summer, because he lives in the city. And in the fall, when the baby comes, he'll go back home."

"I guess that's it," said Martha, "and if he does, maybe they'll stop here on their way home and see us again."

Just then Mrs. Parker came hurrying down the lane and across the road, carrying a jar of hot cherry preserves. Her hair was in wisps about her flushed face, and her apron was covered with cherry stains, but she looked as if she had had a good time.

"Well, children," she said, "I brought some preserves for us to taste for lunch. Did you remember the soup? And was Peter a good boy?"

"Oh, Ma, what do you think happened?" Sally burst out. And she and Martha, and Peter too, began to tell about their guests.

"Well, for goodness sake," said Ma, when she finally understood what they were saying, "to think of that! All those cars stopping because they thought this was a lunch wagon! Come to think of it, there isn't any lunch wagon around here, is there? Well, if we have to make a living, that's one way to do it. But, Sally, I'm not sure

that you should have let a perfect stranger in. But then,
of course you could tell that he was a nice person, and
also he had his little boy with him. Yes, I think you've
got pretty good judgment on the whole. You're a fine
big girl and I'm proud of you." And she took Sally's
face between her sticky hands, and gave her a fine, big
kiss. Then, not wishing to neglect anybody, she did the
same to Martha and Peter.

"Here's the two dollars, Ma," said Sally, feeling very
pleased at the praise.

"You keep that, honey," said her mother. "You certainly earned it, and you do whatever you like with it."

"Oh, Ma, may I really?" Sally had never had so much
money before. She folded it carefully and put it away in
the pocket of her little red handbag. She was rich.

"I guess Ma was right," she thought. "There *is* something good about being the oldest."

15. GEORGE MINDS THE BABY

"**I** SIMPLY must wash clothes today," said Ma, the day after the jam-making. "Pa, will you get some water from the spring, and rig up a clothesline for me?"

"All right," said Pa. "But if you'd wait a few days, we'd get that pipe line laid from the spring and the water wouldn't have to be carried, and you could have all you wanted."

"No, I can't wait," said Ma. "We haven't a clean stitch to put on."

"I'd do it for you today," said Mr. Jefferson, "only I want to get the barn floor fixed so it'll be ready for the cow."

"That's all right," said Ma. "We'll make out fine to-day."

"Well, I'm sorry you have to wash anyhow," said Pa, picking up the two water buckets.

As Mr. Jefferson looked very puzzled, Ma explained: "He used to watch his mother doing the wash when he was young, and he never got over thinking what hard work it was."

"It's just that it doesn't last," said Pa. "Always has to be done over again."

"Good thing it's summer," said Ma. "We don't wear so many clothes."

"I know," said Pa, "but those we do wear get dirtier."

"If we were all cows and horses and dogs and cats," said Ma, "there wouldn't be any washing to do, nor so much talk either." And she began sorting the clothes in piles on the grass. Pa and Bill went up the hill to cut a sapling for a clothes pole, Mr. Jefferson started for the barn, to mix cement for his floor, and Sally started scrubbing the socks in a basin.

George was sitting on the front steps of the car counting the automobiles that slowed down as they passed, and Peter was trying to get into the tub of clothes.

"No," said Sally. "No splashing today. Wash day."

Peter didn't believe her. He lifted his bare foot over the edge of the tub and put it in the water.

"Hot!" he said, looking reproachfully at Sally, as if she had played him a mean trick.

"No, no, Peter," said Sally. "I told you not to. Mother, I don't know what to do with Peter. He wants to get into the tub. Can't George take care of him for once? He isn't doing anything."

"Yes, of course," said Mrs. Parker. "George, you come here and play with your little brother."

"All right, Mama," said George, getting up from the

step. "Come on, Peter, let's play." He picked up a pebble and threw it. "Now Peter throw a stone. See how far you can throw it."

Peter picked up a pebble. He threw it, and it clanked against the side of the washtub.

"Bang!" said Peter.

George threw another pebble far away into the grass, and Peter threw another pebble at the side of the washtub.

"Bang!" he said again, clapping his hands together.

Then he had a better idea. He threw a pebble right into the tub. "Splash!" he said happily. He threw some more pebbles into the tub. If he hadn't shouted "Splash!" so joyfully, Sally might not have noticed him, but after the fourth splash she came to see what was happening.

"No, Peter," she said, crossly. "This is the wash. Don't do that. Mama, George doesn't take care of Peter."

Mrs. Parker put her head out of the window. "George," she called. "Take him a little farther away."

"All right, Ma," said George. "May I take him up to the barn?"

"Yes, if you think you can keep him out of mischief," said his mother. "Put his sandals on. And don't let him get near the horses."

George took Peter's hand and started up the hill with him. They went slowly. It was hard for Peter's short legs to climb over the weeds in the field. At last they reached the barn and sat down in the shade. Peter held up his foot.

"Hurts!" he said.

George took off his sandal and shook the gravel out of it. Through the door they could see Mr. Jefferson smoothing out the wet cement with his trowel.

"Mud!" said Peter. "I want to dig."

"No, no," George told him. "That's not mud. That's cement. Mr. Jefferson is fixing the floor for the cow."

Mr. Jefferson waved his trowel at them. Peter thought this was an invitation to come and play. He jumped up, but George grabbed him.

"Come and see my garden," he said to Peter. He took Peter's hand and led him around to the other side of the barn, where he had his garden.

"Here, you can dig with this," George said, handing Peter a trowel. Peter began to dig right where the seeds were planted.

"No, no, not here," said George. "Over here." He took Peter under the arms and dragged him away from the garden, and sat him down again. Peter began to dig. George remembered that he had not watered his garden that morning.

"Want to water the garden, Peter?" he asked. "You stay right here and dig while I go get some water."

Peter was very busy digging. He didn't even hear what George said. George got a pail from the barn and went to the spring for water.

Peter dug for a few minutes. Then he looked around for George. George wasn't there. Peter got up and walked around. Suddenly he heard a sound. "Cut-cut-cut-cudaaaacut!" He hadn't heard that sound so close for a couple of days. He had grown fond of Mrs. Peck and Mrs. Cluck while they had been tied to the wheel of the trolley car. But they had been taken away and he hadn't been able to find them. He wandered around in the direction of the sound. There, before his eyes, was a wire fence, and behind the fence, not two, but lots of chickens!

"Nice chicken!" said Peter. "Come here, pretty chicken!" He used his most coaxing voice. The chickens were scratching and pecking at the ground, and they weren't tied by strings. At the sound of his voice, some of them bustled over to the fence, sticking their heads forward as they walked and saying, "Cut-cut-cut." They poked their beaks through the fence at Peter's fingers.

"Come out, pretty chicken," said Peter. But the chickens couldn't get out. Peter squatted down and put his hand under the wire. It touched the ground, but Mr. Jefferson had put it up in a hurry and it wasn't stretched very tight, especially where he had used the old wire. Peter lifted the wire. A hen poked her head under.

"Come out," said Peter, pulling at the wire with all his strength. The hen squeezed herself out. Peter stretched out his arms to her. But she walked off, pecking at seeds. Peter started after her, and she went faster.

Peter began to run, as well as he could with only one sandal on. George had forgotten to put the other sandal on again. The hen fled squawking aroung the corner of the barn, with Peter after her. She darted inside.

Mr. Jefferson saw her coming. "How'd that hen get out?" he shouted. Then he saw Peter. "Hey!" Mr. Jefferson called. "Don't you come in here! The cement floor's wet!"

But the hen didn't understand. She was being chased by Peter, and now here was a man who stood up and yelled and waved his arms. She ran as fast as she could, flapping her wings, right across the new cement, and Peter after her, straight out the other door.

By the time George came back with the water, Mr. Jefferson, holding Peter in one arm, was luring the hen back into the chicken yard by sprinkling some grains of corn along the ground. When he had finally got her in, and shut the door, he turned to George.

"You're some baby-nurse," said Mr. Jefferson, "going off and leaving him like that. They must be awful busy down there at the car if they had to put *you* in charge of Peter. Where's his other shoe, now?"

George was surprised. He had thought he was managing very well, minding Peter and watering the garden, and everything.

"What—what did he do?" he asked.

"Look," said Mr. Jefferson, taking George's hand, and leading him around to the cows' part of the barn. "Just look."

There, across the new cement floor, was a row of hen's tracks, clearly printed. And right beside them were the small footprints of a little boy—first a shoe print, and then a bare foot.

George looked scared. "Oh, gosh, Mr. Jefferson, I'm sorry," he said. "Will—will it spoil the floor? I'll help you fix it, honest I will."

Mr. Jefferson laughed. "It's all right," he said. "They weren't either of them heavy enough to spoil the floor. We'll let it go this time. We just won't say anything about it. It'll keep the cow busy, wondering what those marks are and how they got there."

16. A BACK PORCH

NOW THE barn floor was finished, the garden planted, the preserves made, and the wash done. Every day the boys gathered the eggs. On days when there were more than five, the family had eggs for breakfast. On days when there were fewer, Ma made a cake.

Every day Pa and the boys worked in the garden, hoeing and watering and pulling weeds. The beans were poking their curved stems through the earth. Some even had leaves showing. The tomato plants were standing up straight and sprouting new leaves. George watered his own private garden each morning. He didn't mind when the rest of the family laughed at him. When they asked him what he was raising, he just said he hoped it was watermelons.

Pa had got some secondhand pipes and run the water down from the spring, so that they didn't have to go for water.

Mr. Jefferson had promised to build a porch on the

back of the car, and Aunt Hannah said she had a shed that was no use to her, and if Mr. Parker and Mr. Jefferson would take it down, they could have the lumber for their porch.

Every morning and evening Mr. Jefferson went over to help Aunt Hannah with the milking. This had a curious effect on him. He would start jauntily forth, and everybody would be pleased to see him so cheerful. Then he would come back, about an hour later, scowling and silent. If anyone spoke to him, he would mutter something about having to get busy, and then walk away.

"I can't imagine," said Ma, one day, "why it puts him in such a mood to go over there. Anybody'd think he'd enjoy it."

"Maybe he doesn't," said Pa. "Maybe he started and now he doesn't like it, but he thinks he has to keep going."

"I don't think that's it," said Sally. "I think he keeps thinking that pretty soon his vacation will be over and he won't be able to milk the cows any more."

Sally turned out to be partly right.

One morning Mr. Jefferson came back in a very black mood. He sat down on the front step and pulled out his pipe. He jabbed the pipe angrily into his tobacco pouch, and then tried to light it. It wouldn't light. The matches kept going out. After the third try, he threw the matches on the ground and stuck the pipe back into his pocket.

"Asbestos," he muttered.

"Best what?" Sally asked, pausing in her dishwashing.

"Didn't say best anything," Mr. Jefferson growled.

Sally thought it better not to talk any more.

"I said those matches were asbestos," Mr. Jefferson said, loudly. "Won't burn. What's the good of matches that won't burn?" He picked up the matches again and struck one. It burned his finger this time. He uttered something that sounded like a lion's roar and got up and marched off to the barn.

Ma looked after him. "Quick, Sally," she said. "Take him a piece of cake and tell him there's some left-over coffee on the stove." Cake was Ma's cure-all. She cut off a large slice and gave it to Sally, who ran after Mr. Jefferson.

"Ma says to come back and have coffee," she said.

Mr. Jefferson took the cake, bit a piece out of it, turned about, and walked back to the car with Sally. Ma poured out a cup of coffee and set it on the table, with the cream pitcher.

"That's fine cream I've been getting off that milk of Miss Perkins'," she said, craftily.

Mr. Jefferson poured some into his coffee. He took another bite of cake. Then he spoke. "Fine lot of Jersey cows she has there," he said, still scowling. "Shame to sell all that rich milk for cheese."

"I was wondering," said Ma, "why she does that. Seems to me that's good milk for bottling."

"Best milk I ever saw," said Mr. Jefferson. "Barn's no good."

"What's the matter with it?"

"Not sanitary. Can't sell milk except for cheese."

"You mean," Sally asked in surprise, "that it depends what kind of barn you have whether you can sell the milk for milk or for cheese?"

"Sure," scowled Mr. Jefferson. "Milk company won't take milk that's not sanitary. Barn screened. Cement floor. Whitewashed. Scrubbed."

"Would it be better to sell the milk to the milk company?" Mrs. Parker asked.

"Sure. More money."

"Then why doesn't she do it?" Sally asked.

"Hasn't got enough money. Hire help. Fix up the barn."

"Well, now, that is a shame," said Ma, indignantly. "A fine woman like that, struggling along to raise two children, without any help, though I suppose their father does pay board for them. But probably it isn't enough to pay for fixing the barn and putting in screens and hiring help. Now if we could only help her out!"

"Maybe Pa will get a job soon and we'll lend her some money," Sally suggested. "That is," she added doubtfully, "if we have any left over."

"Mm," said Mr. Jefferson. "If." He stood up. "Well, got to be getting busy. Can't sit here all day enjoying myself. Got to get to work."

"What are you going to do today?" Sally asked.

"Start on that porch. Going to make that porch before I leave."

"Oh, that'll be wonderful!" said Sally. "We'll have a whole new room!"

"Hm!" Mr. Jefferson sniffed. He started off again toward the barn.

Sally and her mother watched him from the window. Mrs. Parker shook her head. "It's a shame," she said. "That man ought to stay in the country. He ought to have a dairy farm himself. That's what he wants. What's the good of his driving a milk wagon? A handier man I never saw."

Mr. Jefferson got the horses out and led them across the road to Miss Perkins' barn. Pa and the boys came and helped, and they hitched the horses to Miss Perkins' empty hay wagon. Then they started taking the shed apart. Pa and Mr. Jefferson got up on ladders and started on the roof, prying it up with a crowbar. The roof came off all in one piece, and then they began on the sides, prying off one board at a time. The boys loaded the boards on the wagon. By early afternoon the shed was all taken apart.

As soon as lunch was over, Mr. Jefferson was bound to start work on the porch. He worked with feverish haste. He had to get that porch finished. Pa wanted to take it easy and wait till next day, but Mr. Jefferson wouldn't.

"*I'm* going to start now," he said. So there was nothing for Pa to do but get busy and work too.

First a row of posts had to be driven into the ground to support the beams that had to support the floor.

Mr. Jefferson worked with feverish haste.

"Now what are you going to use for posts?" said Pa. "Thought of that?"

"Fence posts," said Mr. Jefferson, striding to the nearest one and proceeding to pull it up. "You dig the holes to sink them in."

Pa and the boys each took a shovel and dug holes, while Mr. Jefferson pulled up or knocked down one fence post after another. By the end of the afternoon they had a row of posts driven in all along the side of the car away from the road.

Even after supper he insisted on putting some of the beams in place on top of the posts, so that next morning he could start to lay the floor. By noon of the next day the floor was almost all laid, and Pa was putting a railing around the edge. So furiously did they work that by evening the roof was in place. There wasn't enough of the shed roof to make a roof for the whole porch, so they decided to call the part that wasn't roofed a sun deck. It would also be a good place to sit in the evening, when one didn't need shade anyway.

By the end of the day, the old trolley car had a fine new back porch. Ma moved the table and chairs out on it, and the family ate supper there, enjoying the cool breezes and the view of the barn and the vegetable garden.

The porch was also a good place for the water buckets and the washing-up bench. Mr. Jefferson hammered nails along the rail for the family's towels and washcloths, so they could be hung up to dry in the breeze, and that night the children lined up along the porch rail to brush their teeth.

"This certainly is handy," said Bill. "We just dump our toothbrush water overboard."

"I bet I can spit farther than you," said George.

"No, you don't," said Ma, indignantly. "This is a decent household, even if we are out in the country. Kindly pour the water into the pail, and no spitting."

"All right, Ma," said George. "I was only saying I could."

"Well, how do you know you could, if you haven't tried, I'd like to know?" Ma asked. "Probably Bill can. But as you're not going to try, you probably won't find out. Now scoot to bed." And she shooed them indoors. "Sally, what are you doing? Hurry now, you've got to get a good rest before tomorrow."

Sally was in her nightgown, kneeling in the middle of her bed, counting her two dollars. She took them out every night and looked at them, just to make sure they were really there.

"What are we going to do tomorrow, Ma?" she asked.

"It's Saturday and market day," said Ma. "Your father and Mr. Jefferson are going to town, and they've decided to take you with them, for a special treat."

"Oh, Ma! That's wonderful!" Sally cried.

"Are we all going?" Bill asked.

"No, only Sally."

Bill frowned. "Why can Sally go? Why can't we?"

"Because she's the oldest," said Ma. "She gets the first turn. You two will go another time."

"I want to see the farmers' market," said Bill. "Tom was telling me about it. Look, Sally, you take a good look at that farmers' market so you can tell me about it."

"Are you going to spend your two dollars?" George asked.

"Oh, maybe," said Sally. "It depends on what I see."

"You'll probably get some kind of girls' junk," said Bill. "Now if I was going—"

"If I *were* going," Ma corrected. "I wish you children would speak proper English. Anyhow, you're not going. Goodnight, all of you."

She tucked them in, and then she kissed each one goodnight.

When she got to Sally, she felt her neck grabbed in a tight hug. "Thanks, Ma, for letting me go," said Sally.

"I guess you deserve it, honey," said Ma. "But mind you don't buy anything too silly with that money of yours."

Ma went outside to sit on the porch with Pa and Mr. Jefferson, who had their feet up on the rail and were smoking pipes.

"Well," said Ma, as she settled in her chair, "this is certainly a great improvement. It really begins to be like a house, now, with a porch and all."

"All it needs is a chimney," said Pa.

"Wouldn't be hard to make one," said Mr. Jefferson. "Pick up a lot of old bricks, up behind the barn."

"That's right," said Pa. "We could have a stove inside, or maybe even a fireplace. Keep us good and warm in the cold weather."

"No, Pa," Mrs. Parker began. But then she stopped. Pa laughed. "Yes, I know," he said. "You were going to tell me we weren't going to stay here forever, and I should be looking around a bit instead of puttering so much. But you remembered that I'm the boss now, is that it?"

"Well, something like that," Ma said. "But never mind. We can always put a sign out that this is a dining car where we serve lunch. If Sally can do it, so can I."

Sally, looking out through the window from her bed, listened to their voices and felt a little sad. She knew how the grownups felt. Suddenly she thought, "That comes from being the oldest." The boys could hardly wait to be grown up. They were going to do such wonderful things! But Sally had a feeling that it wasn't going to be so easy. When you were little, you thought that grownups could do whatever they liked. But lying there in the twilight, listening to their voices, she knew that they couldn't.

Pa and Mr. Jefferson just wanted to stay out here, milking the cows, or weeding the garden. But Mr. Jefferson had to go back to his job, and Pa would have to find a job soon, and they would all have to go back to town and leave this nice place. And Ma knew that Pa liked farming, and felt sorry that he would have to stop. But they couldn't do as they liked. They had to think of the children. The children had to go to school, and have meals and clothes. So the grownups had to work.

Sally felt like waking the boys up and telling them what she had discovered. But she knew it wouldn't be any use. They were too young.

"Well," she thought, "when I'm big, and make a lot of money, I'll buy a farm and give it to Pa, and he and Ma can enjoy themselves."

But how she would do this, she had no time to figure

out just then. For tomorrow was market day, and she had to go to sleep so as to be up early.

And listening to the grownups' voices, and the chirping of the crickets, Sally fell asleep.

17. TO MARKET

BY EIGHT o'clock the next morning, breakfast was over, the cows were milked, old Whitey was hitched up, and Sally, in her clean starched blue gingham, was ready to go. She had her two dollars in her red handbag. She was going to buy presents for the whole family. She had a package of sandwiches for lunch. Mr. Jefferson came out and boosted her up to the seat, and then jumped up himself. All the family came out to wave good-by. Sally looked down at them from the seat. She felt sorry that Bill couldn't go too. He wanted to so much.

"I'll bring you something nice," she called. Pa came out, putting on his coat, and holding in his teeth the shopping list Ma had given him.

"Don't forget anything that's on the list," Ma called after him, "and don't buy anything that isn't."

"All right, we won't," said Pa, with his teeth clenched on the paper.

He jumped up beside Sally. Mr. Jefferson slapped

the reins on Whitey's back, and they were off at a trot.

All the way to town Sally kept wondering what she would buy. As they got nearer to Taylorville, she looked around at the houses and the people. It seemed ages since she had been in a town, though she knew it was only two weeks. But such a lot of things had happened in that short time!

"I think we'd better stop first at the market," said Pa. "I'd like to get the vegetables and things early."

"All right," said Mr. Jefferson. "You do that while I go on to the hardware store. I'll meet you here, then we'll go to the grocery, and get the cow on the way home."

He pulled up and hitched Whitey to a post on the edge of a large square. In the middle of the square was a large, low building, and all around were stands piled high with vegetables. They all got down and Mr. Jefferson went off to the hardware store. Pa and Sally walked around among the stands.

"What's inside?" Sally asked, pointing to the building.

"That's where they sell meat and bread and things like that. It's a farmers' market. All the farmers come in on Saturday, with everything they have to sell. Now if I were a farmer, that's what I'd do. Come on, let's go inside."

Sally followed him past a lot of counters where ladies were selling chickens and men were selling sides of beef and lamb. Over near the other door was a little counter behind which sat an old lady in a pink knitted shawl. On the counter were pans of fudge and gingerbread.

"Mmmm!" said Sally.

"Let's have some," said Pa.

"Oh, but Pa, it isn't on the list," said Sally.

But Pa bought some anyway. He bought a bag of fudge and three pieces of gingerbread.

"The fudge is for the family," he said. He handed Sally a piece of gingerbread and took a big bite out of another piece. The third he put in his pocket for Mr. Jefferson.

They went out again, and Pa began buying vegetables.

"Wish I'd got that garden in sooner," he said. "Wouldn't have to pay good money for all this stuff."

"Oh, but Pa, you couldn't help it," said Sally. "Why, two weeks ago you didn't even know you were going to have a garden at all! Look, look, Pa. See what that boy has!"

Sally pulled her father's sleeve. She pointed to a boy who stood beside a box. One side of the box was of chicken wire. Inside, something brown and furry was moving. Sally peeped in. Two little brown rabbits were huddled together in a corner of the box.

"Oh, what darling rabbits," Sally exclaimed. "Are you going to sell them?"

"Mebbe," said the boy.

"What do you mean, mebbe?" Sally asked.

"Mebbe somebody'll buy 'em," said the boy. "And mebbe not."

Pa smiled and went back to the vegetables.

"Can I touch them?" Sally asked.

The boy lifted the top of the box, and Sally put her hand on one of the rabbits.

She had an idea. Maybe she could buy one for Bill!

"How much do they cost?" she asked. She knew she shouldn't. Perhaps the boy would say they were two dollars apiece. Then of course she couldn't.

"Dollar," he said, pursing his lips and sticking his hands deep in his pockets.

"For one?" Sally asked.

"No, both," said the boy.

"Is that all?"

"All they're wuth," said the boy.

Sally suddenly decided. "I'll take them," she said, opening her purse. She pulled out one of the dollar bills and handed it to the boy. "Pa," she called. "Look, Pa, see what I bought!"

Pa turned from the vegetables to see what she was talking about.

"It's in here," said Sally, pointing to the box. Pa peered inside at the frightened rabbits. "The boy sold them to me. Is it all right? One for George and one for Bill. I paid him a dollar."

"But, Sally," said Pa, "rabbits aren't on the list."

"I know," said Sally, "but aren't they cute?"

"They're cute, all right," her father admitted. "But what will you feed them? And how are you going to get them home?"

"I don't know," said Sally.

The boy stuffed the dollar into his pocket and said, "You kin have the box."

"All right," said Pa. "That's mighty nice of you, Mister. I couldn't think how we'd get them home, hopping around in the bottom of a milk wagon, but if you don't need the box, I guess we can manage." He winked at Sally. "Soon as we get home, we'll pass the fudge around. Then show Ma the rabbits later. But look, if those rabbits get into my garden, out they go, hear?"

"Oh, they won't," said Sally, "we'll build them a fence."

"They'll dig underneath," the boy said.

"That's right," said Pa. "You've got to watch them. Soon as they get out, bing, that's the end of them. Rabbit stew."

"Oh, Pa! You wouldn't do that!" said Sally reproachfully.

They carried the rabbits and the vegetables to the wagon and loaded them in the back, and waited for Mr. Jefferson.

When he arrived, Pa said, "Now we have to buy the groceries."

"It's getting warm," said Mr. Jefferson. "How about some ice cream cones?"

"That would be wonderful," Sally said, "but I'd feel

bad about the boys not having any. If we could only take them some!"

"Now don't you worry about the boys," Pa said. "They'll have their turn."

On the way they passed fascinating shop windows. Sally looked in all of them for presents for the rest of the family. But she had only a dollar left. It was funny —the two dollars had looked so big when the man had given them to her; she had felt so rich, and now it didn't seem as if she would have enough. There was a nice teddy bear that Peter would like, but it was marked two dollars. And here were some lovely aprons, but they were seventy-nine cents!

At last her eyes brightened. "Look, Pa," she said, "here's the ten-cent store. May I stop here and do some shopping?"

"All right," said Pa. "I still have to get the groceries."

"I have some errands too," said Mr. Jefferson. "Say we leave Sally here and come back in half an hour."

"I never knew a woman to buy everything she wanted in the ten-cent store in half an hour," said Pa, "but then, she only has a dollar left. Maybe half an hour will be enough."

Sally went into the ten-cent store by herself. She felt very grown up indeed. She looked at the toothbrushes and washcloths, with a businesslike air.

"Can I help you, miss?" the saleslady asked.

"No, thank you," said Sally, and walked on. She didn't want toothbrushes! But it was nice to be called "Miss."

Then she came to the glassware. There was a beautiful red glass pitcher that she thought Ma would like. That was fifteen cents. Then she found a string of blue glass beads that would do for Aunt Hannah. They shone with all the colors of the rainbow when you held them up to the light. They would go with any dress Aunt Hannah put on.

A little farther on she found some bandanna handkerchiefs. Pa and Mr. Jefferson would each like one. They could wear them around their necks, or keep them in their pockets with a corner sticking out, and they would look more like farmers.

Then at the toy counter she found a green and yellow ball for Peter, and for Martha, two tiny doll babies wrapped in a bit of blue flannel.

"She'll like them," Sally thought. "I'll help her to make some tiny little clothes for them."

Now she passed a counter that had things for animals. There was a little gray cloth mouse.

"What's that for?" she asked the saleslady.

"That's a catnip mouse, miss," said the saleslady. "For cats to play with. Makes them roll over and act silly."

"I'll get one for Kinky," Sally said. "How much are they?"

"Five cents for the little ones, and ten for the big ones."

"Kinky is a very small cat," said Sally. "I'll take a little one."

Then she noticed some eggs. What on earth were they

doing with eggs in the ten-cent store? They looked smooth and shiny and milky-white. They were glass eggs!

"I'll have some fun with one of these," said Sally. "I'll put one in a nest, and Ma will think the hen laid some new kind of egg. And here are some iron bells. I guess they're cowbells."

She bought one for Mr. Jefferson's new cow that they were going to get. And now she had only fifteen cents left, and she hadn't bought anything for Tom.

She couldn't think what to get Tom. He was too big for toys, and a boy wouldn't care anything for a pair of socks or a handkerchief. Candy wouldn't last long, and besides, she couldn't get enough to share. She walked slowly toward the door.

Suddenly her eye was caught by a sign. "Play the flute. Learn music and amuse your friends." On the counter were some tin pipes.

"Why, that's just the thing," she said. "I bet Tom will be able to play one of those." And she handed over her last fifteen cents and took the long thin package.

And now all her money was gone and she was back at the door with her arms full of packages. But where was Pa and where was Mr. Jefferson? Surely she hadn't taken more than half an hour! She waited anxiously. Of course they wouldn't go home without her, but Pa had said half an hour and now he wasn't here.

At last she saw him, hurrying down the street. He waved to her.

"Why, Pa, you're late," said Sally. "You said you always had to wait for a woman to shop, and now I had to wait for you." She grinned at him.

"Well, I did have to wait for a woman," said Pa. "That girl in the grocery store took so long to wrap up my things, I thought I'd be there all night. Where's Mr. Jefferson?"

"Here he comes," said Sally.

Mr. Jefferson had a package in one hand and three ice cream cones in the other. He held out the cones to Sally and said, "Here, take your choice."

As Sally couldn't take anything without dropping her packages, she opened her mouth and took a lick of the nearest cone.

"Here, put your bundles in my pockets," said Pa, taking them from her.

"What's in your package, Mr. Jefferson?" Sally asked.

"Surprise," he said, winking at her, as they walked back to the milk wagon.

On the way home they stopped for the cow, at the farm where Mr. Jefferson had arranged to buy her. The farmer led her out and tied her to the back of the wagon. She was a pretty brown and white cow, with little curling horns. When she was tied up, she turned her head around in a puzzled way and said "Moooooo," as if she couldn't understand why she was being led off in the middle of the day when she was just starting to chew her cud.

"So long, Bess," said the farmer. "Be a good girl." And they started off.

18. A NEST EGG

THEY HAD to go slowly now, on account of the cow. "Mustn't hurry a cow," said Mr. Jefferson. "Spoil the milk."

So it was well along in the afternoon when they finally came in sight of the trolley car. All the family, as well as the Perkinses, were out to greet them as they turned in at the lane.

Bill hurried to untie the cow and lead her to the spring for a drink. Tom unhitched Whitey and led him off for a drink too, and the others took the packages Pa handed down from the wagon and carried them up on the porch. And all the while there was a chorus of questions. "Did you have a good time? Did you get everything? What did you bring me? Was there a big crowd? Did you have ice cream?"

George wanted to know what Sally had bought with her two dollars, but she wouldn't tell him.

"I'm going to wait till everybody sits down together," she said. "Then I'll show you all together."

Ma sent George off to put the meat in the spring, and when the boys had all returned, Pa handed round the fudge. Then, while they all sat munching it, Sally brought out her presents. She handed out one at a time, so that everybody could see each present as it was unwrapped.

Ma's was first. She kissed Sally and hugged her, and put the red glass pitcher in the middle of the table to hold flowers. Aunt Hannah put on her beads, and Pa and Mr. Jefferson tied their bandannas round their necks. Mr. Jefferson was going to tie the cowbell around his neck too, but when he was told it was for the cow, he was just as pleased. Bill ran down and tied it on her and it tinkled softly as she chewed her cud under a tree.

Martha loved her little doll babies. Peter rolled his ball off the porch and nearly fell off after it, and Kinky was so silly with his catnip mouse that George took it away from him for fear he would have a fit. Then poor Kinky miaowed and searched all around for the mouse, and sniffed the floor where he had rolled with it, and George felt so sorry for him that he had to give it back.

As soon as Tom had unwrapped his tootle pipe he put it to his lips and played Yankee Doodle.

"Jumping grasshoppers!" he exclaimed. "How did you know what I wanted? This is swell!"

"I thought you wanted a fiddle," said Sally.

"Sure, but if I can't have a fiddle, a pipe is the next best thing," said Tom.

Bill and George sat and watched. There didn't seem to be anything for them. They didn't want to ask, but they were wondering whether Sally had spent all her money on the other presents, or whether she had decided to keep some for herself, and just hadn't brought them anything.

Suddenly there was a scratching, shuffling noise inside the wagon.

"What's that?" Bill asked.

"Oh," said Sally, "I almost forgot. Your present and George's present are in there. Better get them quick."

Bill and George ran off to the wagon. When they came back carrying the box with the two rabbits, they could hardly speak for joy and surprise.

"Is—is that what you got for us?" said Bill when he could talk. "Gosh, Sally, thanks!"

"It's the best present of all!" said George.

"I knew you'd like them," said Sally. "They were so cute I couldn't help buying them."

Then she looked at her mother. Ma was staring at the rabbits, looking hopeless and exasperated at the same time. It seemed you couldn't trust a Parker to go anywhere and not bring back some kind of livestock.

"I know they weren't on the list," said Sally, "but I forgot, until after I'd bought them."

"I told her," said Pa, trying to look stern. "I warned her, but she'd bought them already. So it was too late. Now, boys, get them some water and some fresh grass.

And you'll have to build them a good strong pen. For as I told Sally, the first time they get out and eat the garden, that's the end of them. Rabbit stew."

"Oh, Pa, we couldn't eat them," said Bill.

"Oh, yes, we could," said Pa. "Rabbit meat tastes good. Ummmmm!" and he licked his lips over an imaginary morsel of something good.

At this Aunt Hannah got up. "Mr. Parker is hungry," she said. "And you're all having supper at my house tonight. So I'll be going now, to get everything ready, and you folks come as soon as you can."

She took Martha's hand and departed, and Tom followed, tootling on his new pipe.

Ma began to put away the groceries, and Pa and the boys and Mr. Jefferson went up to the barn to do the chores. Bill had his first chance to milk Bess, the new cow, while Mr. Jefferson watched to see that he did it right.

Mr. Jefferson was very approving. "You'll make a fine dairy man some day," he said, patting Bill on the back, and Bill grinned proudly up at him.

When the family was ready to start across the road, Sally suddenly remembered something.

"You all go on ahead," she said, "I forgot something. I'll catch up with you right away."

It was the glass egg, which she had put in her red purse. She ran as fast as she could to the barn and put the egg in one of the nests in the chickens' room. Then she ran back and caught up with the family.

The supper at Aunt Hannah's house was to be a farewell feast for Mr. Jefferson. Tomorrow he had to start back to East Sawyerville, for his two weeks were over. And on Monday morning he had to go back to work.

Aunt Hannah said it was a long time since so many people had eaten at her table, and it should have been a gay party. But instead it was the gloomiest gathering that had ever sat down to such a good dinner. To be sure, they all had good appetites. But the children looked solemn as they emptied their plates. The grownups looked sad, and Mr. Jefferson positively scowled. He looked crosser than he used to look at seven o'clock in the morning in East Sawyerville. He didn't say a word. Nobody else said much either.

Finally, when the pie was brought in, Pa felt called upon to say something.

"Well, Mr. Jefferson," he observed, "we certainly will miss you." Then he sighed. "In fact, I don't know what we are going to do without you." Mr. Jefferson still didn't say a word. He watched Aunt Hannah cut the pie.

Ma said, "You've been a good friend to us, and I wish you could see your way to staying as a member of the family. Maybe we could even adopt you, though I've never heard of such a thing being done with a grown-up man."

Mr. Jefferson muttered, "Excuse me a minute." Then he got up and went out of the dining room.

Ma was alarmed. "Maybe I shouldn't have said that," she said. "Maybe he didn't like it."

But at that moment Mr. Jefferson came back, holding the package he had brought from town. He hadn't said what was in it, and now he placed it on the table in front of Aunt Hannah.

"Thought this would go nice with the pie," he mumbled, as he took off the paper, and revealed a box of ice cream.

"Ice cream!" Aunt Hannah exclaimed. "But how on earth could you keep it so long?"

"Dry ice," said Mr. Jefferson. He picked up a spoon and fished out from among the wrappings several little blocks of something white, which he put on a plate. The little blocks steamed faintly.

"Don't touch them," said Mr. Jefferson, as the children reached out to feel the dry ice. "Burn yourself."

"Well, that's the most remarkable thing I ever saw," said Aunt Hannah.

"Just imagine," said Ma, "having ice cream way out here in the country where we don't even have gas and electricity!"

"Now, Ma," said Pa. "How many times do I have to tell you that we're only five miles from Taylorville—"

Everybody laughed. It was always funny when Pa got out of patience because Ma insisted that they were out in the wilderness. After that the talk was more cheerful, and though Mr. Jefferson still didn't say much, and Aunt Hannah herself sighed now and then, there was a more festive air as they ate pie and ice cream. There were three quarts of ice cream, and everybody, even the boys, had as much as they could hold.

But when the Parkers were at home again, they couldn't help going back to being sad. They didn't feel like talking much. Mr. Jefferson was so much a part of the family, and they had had such a good time with him! Absent-mindedly, Ma put little Peter to bed. Sally sat stroking the kitten. Since they hadn't cooked dinner, there were no dishes to wash, and the chores were all done, so they just sat around and kept quiet.

Finally George got up. "I'm going to have a look at the rabbits," he said, and he wandered off to the barn.

In a little while he came running back. "Look what I found!" he shouted. "What a funny egg! I guess a hen just laid it, because it's warm! Look, Pa!"

He held out to his father the glass egg. Sally giggled. The others gathered around to see the strange egg.

"Maybe we're giving them the wrong kind of feed," said Bill, anxiously.

"Now, see here," said Pa, laughing, "a hen couldn't lay an egg like that!"

"But I went in to see if there were any eggs," said George, "and Mrs. Cluck jumped down out of the box and there was this egg. It's warm!"

"That's a glass egg," said Pa. "Who put that egg in there?"

Sally giggled again. "I did, Pa," she confessed. "I bought it in town, and I put it in there for fun, because

George came running back.

I thought somebody would find it and get fooled. And Georgie did!"

"Don't you know what that's for?" Pa asked.

Sally shook her head. "I didn't know it was for anything, except to have some fun with," she said.

"It's a nest egg," Pa explained. "You put it in the nest to get the hen to set. Then she lays some more eggs, and sets on them till they hatch. Want to raise some chicks, Sally?"

"Sure," said Sally. "Chicks are cute."

Ma groaned. "Oh, dear! More animals!"

"Well, Mary," said Pa, "it looks as if we have a family of farmers, and we'll just have to figure out some way to keep this farm going. We can't let that nest egg go to waste."

"No, indeed," said Sally. "I'm going to go right back and put it back in the nest." And she took the egg and ran to the barn.

19. SAD SUNDAY

THE NEXT day Mr. Jefferson milked the cows for the last time. He was going to make an early start, for he would have to begin work very early Monday morning, and he wanted to get a nap when he got home.

"It's going to be hard getting back into the old rut again," he said at breakfast. "'Tain't natural for a man to work in the dark and sleep in the daytime. It took me a long time to learn to do it, and now in this short time I've got all out of the habit."

Mrs. Parker busied herself packing him a good lunch, and she put enough into the basket to last for supper too, for she said a man all alone wasn't likely to get himself any sort of meal when he got home to an empty house.

"I wonder how Whitey will like his stable," said Bill.

"I guess he won't like it," said Mr. Jefferson. "He won't like his job either. He's had a vacation too, roaming around in the field and sleeping at night like a respectable horse."

Whitey had even gotten used to the sun, and had been going without his hat, but when Mr. Jefferson hitched him up, he put the hat on him.

"He might as well get used to being a night horse again," he said.

When all was ready, the Parkers and the Perkinses gathered in front of the trolley car to watch Mr. Jefferson depart. The borrowed horse was tied on behind the milk wagon. Whitey wiggled his ears through the holes in his hat.

Bill put his arm around Whitey's neck and rubbed his long white nose. Then he pulled a lump of sugar out of his pocket. Whitey's big soft lips nuzzled Bill's hand as he crunched the sugar.

"Good-by, Whitey," Bill whispered miserably.

"Good-by," Mr. Jefferson called, waving his hand sadly. Then he slapped the reins on Whitey's back. Whitey turned his head and looked back at the Parkers and the Perkinses. Then he started off, clop, clop, down the road.

Ma wiped her eyes with her apron and said, "Well, I guess those dishes won't wash themselves," and turned back to the car.

"I'll help you," said Aunt Hannah, following her.

"Guess I'll go up and look at the garden," said Pa.

"I'll go along and see the rabbits," said Bill.

George went too, to see his garden. Pa's garden was

It seemed to be some sort of vine.

growing in neat rows of green now, and the little corn shoots were about four inches high. But the amazing thing was George's garden. Something was growing there, but nobody knew what it was. George watered it every day, and kept the earth soft and loose and the weeds down, and every day there were a few more leaves. It seemed to be some sort of vine, but whether it was squash or cucumber, or what it was, nobody knew for sure.

When they asked George, he said watermelons. Nobody knew how he could tell, but he kept hoping it was watermelons.

Bill and George wandered about the barn. The rabbits were munching some carrot tops in their cage. The hens were scratching in their yard.

Suddenly George said, "Sh! Look at that hen."

It was Mrs. Cluck, the black hen. She was sitting in the nest where Sally had put the glass egg. As they stood watching her, she flopped out of the box and waddled off to get a drink. Bill and George peered in. There were two eggs in the box. One was the glass egg and one was a real one.

"She laid it!" said Bill.

"What's so wonderful about that? She's always laying eggs," said George.

"Yes, but don't you see? She was sitting on it! Maybe she's going to lay some more and hatch them!"

"That's right," George whispered. "Come on, let's tell Sally."

They ran down to the car and yelled, "Mrs. Cluck laid an egg! Right in the nest with the glass egg! She's going to have a nest!"

The family were so pleased about Mrs. Cluck, that they began to feel better about Mr. Jefferson.

"We must write him a letter," Sally said. "If she lays another egg by tomorrow, we'll know it's true and then we'll tell him."

That evening, as they all sat at supper on the porch, Bill suddenly remembered something.

"You know," he said, "before we came here we were planning to play baseball."

"Yes, and go swimming," Sally added. "Remember, Ma said she wouldn't have to wash us so much if we went swimming?"

"We've just been too gosh-darned busy," said Bill, stuffing a piece of cake into his mouth. "Excuse me, please, I have to go and milk Bess."

"And I have to feed the rabbits," said George.

"And I have to feed the chickens," said Sally.

Pa looked after them as they went up the hill. "It's good for them to be out here," he said.

"It certainly is," said Ma, picking up the sleepy Peter and carrying him off to bed. "They're getting brown, and I think they're getting fat. Have you noticed their appetites?"

"That's one thing that was worrying me," said Pa. "I've got to figure out some way to keep them all fed."

20. PA DECIDES

THE DAYS passed quickly. They were all so busy, they just didn't know where the time went. Mrs. Cluck laid more eggs, ten of them, and she sat on her nest like a good mother, only getting off it to eat the tidbits that Sally brought her, and to walk around a bit. The garden grew, and so did the weeds. There was butter to be made, now that they had Bess. And when there was any time to spare, Aunt Hannah could always use a bit of help.

But Pa was getting more and more uneasy. A couple of times a week he rode off on his bicycle to town, to see about jobs, and to bring back groceries. There were plenty of groceries to be had, but no jobs. The family didn't like to talk about it, because of the way Pa felt. He wanted to stay here, but it looked very much as if they might have to go back to East Sawyerville. Worst of all, it looked as if Pa might have to take the job driving a bus, which they all knew he didn't want to do.

"I wish there were something we could do," said Sally

one day. "I keep wishing and wishing, but I can't think of anything."

"We could put out a sign and let people stop and have lunch the way you did that time," George suggested.

"I guess we could," Sally said, "but Pa wouldn't like that. It wouldn't be his job. I suppose we could pray hard. Or we could wish on the first star every night. I've tried that, but maybe if we all did it something would happen."

"Let's get Tom and Martha too," said George, "and all of us wish together."

That evening, as soon as the first pale star appeared, all five children stopped still in their tracks and began whispering.

> "Star light, star bright,
> First star I see tonight,
> Wish I may, wish I might
> Have the wish I wish tonight."

Of course they all wished the same thing. They wished on the first star every night for a week, but nothing happened.

Then George had an idea. "Ma," he said, one day at dinner, "couldn't we have chicken some time?"

His mother stared at him. "Why, I don't know," she said. "The hens are all laying. We couldn't kill one now. What ever put that into your head?"

"Oh, I just thought it would be nice," he said.

"Well, we may come to it, but I hope not," said Ma.

Sally stared at him too. After dinner she took him aside and asked, "What came over you, asking for chicken?"

"Oh, I was just thinking we could wish on a wishbone if we had a wishbone," he said. "Then the two people who were pulling would be wishing the same thing, so whoever got their wish it would be all right."

"Well, it was a good idea," said Sally. "Let's see, some people wish on the first fruit they eat."

George thought about that, and a little later he went up to the orchard. The only fruit he could find was a green apple. He bravely took a bite, wishing hard as he forced himself to chew and swallow it.

"I wish Pa would get a nice job that he would like and I wish we could stay here," he murmured. "I wonder if I have to eat this whole thing or would a couple of bites be enough?"

He decided that half the apple would be fair, but it was pretty sour. He went back to the trolley car and asked for a piece of bread. It was to take away the taste of the apple, but he didn't tell that to Ma. She would have given him a scolding and some milk of magnesia.

At last the day came when Ma decided she had to do something. Their money was almost gone and she was going to earn some. Right after breakfast she got out her mixing bowls and baking powder and flour and milk.

"Run and get me some eggs," she commanded. Bill asked no questions, but ran to the hen house.

"What are you going to do, Ma?" Sally asked.

"I'm going to make some cakes," said Mrs. Parker, "and I'm going to put them outside in the china closet and put up a sign and maybe sell them."

"Why, Ma!" Sally exclaimed. She felt alarmed. If Ma was going to put her precious china closet outside, things must be getting pretty bad. "I'll help you," she said.

"You just keep Peter out from under my feet," said Ma, "and I'll make the cakes myself. Oh, and Sally, do you think you can hang up the clothes?"

Ma had washed the day before, but it had rained before she got the clothes hung up, and she had left them soaking in cold water overnight. Today was clear and sunny, and very windy.

"A good drying day," Ma said. "Be sure and push those pins on tight, Sally."

Sally went out and began to hang up the clothes. It seemed to get windier all the time. The wind almost tore the clothes out of her hands. It was all she could do to get them on the line.

Things began to go wrong that day, right from the start, and probably it was all because of the wind. George bumped into Bill as he came running down from the barn with the eggs. When they picked themselves up, four eggs were broken. That made Ma pretty cross. Then the kitten jumped at a corner of the tablecloth and upset a cup of milk.

Then the wind blew the flame of the kerosene stove so that the oven wouldn't heat up properly.

Then, when Sally had finally got most of the clothes hung up, a terrific gust of wind came along and broke the line. Snap, there it lay on the ground, with all the clean clothes in the dust, and then the wind began to whip at the clothes. The clothespins came off and the clothes blew every which way. Bill and Sally and George ran about picking them up. The bushes were decorated with underwear and socks. By the time they were all gathered up and put back in the tub to be washed over again, the first batch of cakes was done.

"Now everybody keep out of here," said Ma, "or something terrible will happen," and she went to take the cakes out of the oven. But Peter came up behind and pushed her, and she burned her hand against the stove and dropped the very best layer.

"Sally, *will* you take this child out of here!" Ma called.

Peter was not used to hearing his mother speak so crossly. He began to cry. Ma was on her knees picking up the broken pieces of cake and muttering to herself, when Pa came down from the garden. He was cross too.

"Where's Bill?" he demanded.

"Here I am, Pa," said Bill.

"I told you to watch those rabbits," said Pa. "They got out of the cage. They've eaten three tomato plants and I don't know how many beans."

"Oh, my gosh," said Bill, starting for the barn at a run.

"I'm going to get rid of those rabbits," said Pa. "I don't know what we want rabbits for anyway."

"Isn't that what I've been telling you?" Ma demanded.

"Did they eat *my* garden?" George asked, tearfully.

"I don't know whether they did or not," said Pa. "What's all this cake-baking going on here?"

"Ma's going to put the cakes in the china closet," said Sally, "and sell them."

"You are not," said Pa. "I'll not have any such goings on!"

"Why, Pa!" said Mrs. Parker. "What's come over you? Why shouldn't I, if I want to?"

Pa walked over to the table and banged his fist on it. "Because I say so," he said loudly. "This can't go on any longer. I have made up my mind!" And he stalked out of the car and started toward the barn.

"Where are you going?" Ma called after him.

"I'm going for my bicycle," Pa called back over his shoulder. "And then I'm going to East Sawyerville, and I'm going to get a job."

Ma and Sally ran after him. "What kind of job?" Ma demanded. "What do you mean?"

Pa stopped walking and looked at them. Then he spoke in a quieter voice. "I'm going to get a job driving a bus," he said. "I've been thinking about it. It's a mighty good job and it's just downright silly of me not to take it."

"But Pa, you don't like busses," said Sally.

"Well, honey, I guess I can get used to them," said Pa. "Now don't you worry. I'll be back by night. When I come back we'll know what's going to happen, and then we'll make plans."

He went on to the barn, and soon came back with his bicycle, which he wheeled out to the road.

"Wait, Pa," said Mrs. Parker. "Wait till I fix you some lunch." She ran back to the kitchen and began to make sandwiches. "Thank goodness we have plenty of cake," she said, "even if it isn't frosted yet." And she cut one of the large layers in half and wrapped it in paper.

They all stood by the side of the road and watched Pa as he mounted his bicycle and started off. "So long," he called. "Don't look for me too early. Good-by."

"Good-by, Pa," the children called. Ma was wiping her eyes with her apron, as she had done when Mr. Jefferson left. Sally and Bill and George looked solemnly at each other. It seemed as if one part of their wish was coming true. But what about the other part?

21. MR. JEFFERSON HAS ALSO DECIDED

MRS. PARKER went back inside to clear up the mess, and to put water on to wash the clothes.

The children sat by the side of the road talking.

"I never saw Pa act like that," said George. "He was real mad, wasn't he?"

"I don't think so, really," said Sally. "He just acted that way because he felt bad."

Bill grinned. "I thought I'd die laughing when I saw Sally running all over after those clothes."

"You'd laugh on the other side of your face if you had to wash them," said Sally, looking around to see where Ma was. Her mother didn't like her to say that.

"And Ma dropping the cake, and Pa getting mad about the rabbits," said George, giggling.

"Never mind laughing at those rabbits," said Bill. "I have to make a new cage. They dug out underneath."

"You'd better do it today," said Sally. "But I guess if we're going away it won't matter," she finished sadly. "I wonder what's going to happen."

Tom and Martha came over just then, and saw them sitting there. "What are you doing?" Tom asked.

"Pa just went to town to get a job driving a bus," said Sally. "Maybe we'll have to go away."

"Go away?" said Martha. "You can't! I won't let you!" She looked so fierce that they all laughed.

Suddenly Bill jumped to his feet. "Look!" he shouted. "Look there!" and he pointed down the road.

"What is it?" they cried. And then they saw. It was a horse and wagon. It was coming toward them. The horse was wearing a little straw sun hat. Could it be— It was!

"It's Mr. Jefferson!" they screamed. "He's coming back! Hooray!" Their yells brought Ma to the window.

"What on earth is the matter with you children, yelling and screaming like that?"

"Look, Ma," they cried. "It's Mr. Jefferson!" The wagon came nearer, and drew up to a stop right in front of the car, and Mr. Jefferson shouted "Whoa!" and jumped to the ground.

"Mr. Jefferson!" the children squealed, dancing around him in their joy. Sally flung her arms around his neck and gave him a big kiss.

"Well!" he said. "That's the best welcome a man ever had. Sure is nice to come back to friends."

Whitey wagged his head up and down and whinnied. He was glad to be back too. Bill hugged the horse's neck and rubbed his nose.

Ma said, "This is the pleasantest surprise I could have asked for. Have you come for a good long visit?"

"No, ma'am," said Mr. Jefferson, smiling, "I've come to stay!"

"To stay! That's swell!" And all five children began to do a war dance around him.

"I couldn't stand it," he said. "It was too lonesome. Too quiet. No kids yelling and screaming. No chickens. No cows."

"But your job!" said Ma.

"Gave it up," said Mr. Jefferson. "What do I want it for? Took my money out of the bank." He patted his pocket. "Got it right here. I'm going into the dairy business."

Then he looked at Tom and Martha. "Where's your Aunt Hannah?" he asked sharply. "I've got to see her right away."

And he started off across the road.

"No, wait," said Ma. "Let Tom go and ask her to come here. We can't let you go again till we've talked a little more."

"Sure," said Tom, and was off like a bullet out of a gun.

They all went up on the porch and sat down.

"Where's Mr. Parker?" Mr. Jefferson asked.

"He's gone to town for a job," said Ma. "Didn't you pass him on the road? He was riding his bicycle."

Mr. Jefferson looked puzzled. "No, I didn't see him. Wait. Seems to me I did see a man on a bicycle. But I didn't recognize him. Man was riding fast, with his head down. It must have been Mr. Parker, but I didn't know him."

"It's funny he didn't see you, or anyway recognize the wagon," said Ma.

"Well, that's not so funny," said Mr. Jefferson. "Didn't you notice the wagon? I painted it." They looked out of the window. Sure enough, the wagon was painted brown. It really didn't look like a milk wagon at all.

"Wouldn't it be too bad if we had to go back to town just when you've come back to stay?" said Sally.

"Well, we'll not say anything about that till your father comes back," said Ma. "We'll wait and see what he says."

Just then Tom and Aunt Hannah came hurrying across the road. Aunt Hannah's cheeks were pink and her eyes were shining. She had her apron on and she was drying her hands on it as she came. She was quite excited.

"How do, Miss Hannah," said Mr. Jefferson, jumping down off the porch and holding out his hand. "I've come back to stay. I'm going into the dairy business."

"That's—that's wonderful!" said Aunt Hannah. "I'm so glad to see you!"

"Come up and sit down, everybody," said Ma. "We'll all have milk and cake. Thank goodness there's plenty of cake." And she began to cut large pieces, and to pour out milk.

Mr. Jefferson and Aunt Hannah were sitting and talking together excitedly. The children were all shouting

"I've come to stay!"

and talking at once. Suddenly Mr. Jefferson held up his hand for silence.

"Just a minute, everybody," he said. "I want to tell you something. Miss Hannah and I have just decided something. We're going into the dairy business together. We're going to be partners."

The children didn't quite understand what all this meant. But Ma looked at Aunt Hannah and then at Mr. Jefferson and said, "Well, bless my soul!" in the queerest voice.

And Aunt Hannah looked back at Ma and got very red in the face.

"Why, that's wonderful," said Ma, at last. "I'm sure I couldn't think of a better arrangement. I wish Pa were here. I can't wait to tell him."

"Thank you," said Mr. Jefferson. "I think it's a pretty good arrangement myself."

22. WISHES COME TRUE

THE AFTERNOON was spent in a tour of the place. All the Parkers had to take Mr. Jefferson to see what had been done in his absence, and the Perkinses went too.

They went first to the pasture, for Mr. Jefferson wanted to see his cow. He found her in fine condition, and said that Bill would make a first class dairy man.

Then they went to the barn to inspect the poultry. Mrs. Cluck was sitting on her nest like a good mother hen. The other chickens were taking an afternoon snooze in the dust of the chicken yard.

Mr. Jefferson was properly amazed at the garden. It had grown splendidly. The boys had hoed it so well that there was not a single weed. The tomato plants had little green tomatoes on them, the beans were blossoming, and the corn was nearly two feet high.

"You certainly have done wonders," said Mr. Jefferson. "I bet you water those plants with milk to make them grow like that."

"We do not!" said Sally. "We make cheese and butter, and *I* think we ought to get a pig to drink up the skim milk."

"Well, now, that's a good idea!" said Mr. Jefferson.

But before he could say another word about buying more livestock, Ma interrupted. "Let's go back now," she said. "I think you've seen about all there is to see."

But George protested loudly. "No! You haven't seen my private garden yet! Come and look at my watermelon patch." And he grabbed Mr. Jefferson's hand and pulled him around behind the barn, waving at the others to come too.

"Well, look at that!" said Mr. Jefferson. "Now what do you call that?"

Flourishing vines trailed over the ground, with big healthy leaves and yellow blossoms. George had certainly taken good care of his garden. The ground was soft and well watered, and there was a little fence of sticks around it.

"It's even got one watermelon," said George, flopping to his knees to show a little green knob with a bit of blossom still sticking to it.

"That's no watermelon," said Tom.

"Well, what is it then?" George asked.

"It's pumpkin," said Tom.

"So it is," said Aunt Hannah.

"Well, that's nice," said Tom. "We didn't plant any pumpkins this year. You get your Ma to make pumpkin pie. It's my favorite."

"Say!" Mr. Jefferson said. "Where'd you get the seeds? Weren't those the seeds you found in the barn one day in an old tin can?"

"That's right," said George. "And Pa said they wouldn't grow, because they were five years old at least. Wait'll I tell him. Wait'll he sees my pumpkin vine!"

Tom burst out laughing. "Ha! What do you mean five years? You find those seeds in the barn in an old tin can? I left them there myself just last spring."

"And that's why we didn't plant pumpkins!" said Martha. "Because you couldn't remember where you put the seeds!"

Tom yanked one of his sister's pigtails and said, "Hey! what's the idea, telling tales about me?" And Martha turned red and hid behind her Aunt Hannah.

"Well, it's a good joke on us," said Ma, as they walked back along the lane. "We thought we were such good farmers we could even get watermelons out of pumpkin seeds five years old."

"No, Ma, that's not right," said George.

"Well, never mind," said Ma. "I'm so happy I'm a little mixed up. I only wish Pa were here. But I don't look for him till late. It's a long ride on a bicycle, and the poor man will be tired out when he does get here. I can't wait to see his face when he comes in tonight and sees Mr. Jefferson sitting here, and his bed made up the way it was when we first came."

Here Aunt Hannah, gently but firmly, announced her intention of having Mr. Jefferson occupy the spare bed-

room in her house. As they were going into business together, it stood to reason that he should be right there
on the premises.

At this the Parker children protested that Mr. Jefferson belonged to them, and the Perkins children said that
the Parkers had had their turn, and now he belonged to
them. They were getting as near to an argument as they
had ever been, when a big truck stopped in the road.

"What's this?" said Ma. "If anybody wants lunch
served, tell them we changed our minds."

But somebody was getting down from the truck.

"Jumping catfish!" Bill shouted. "It's Pa!"

"But what's he doing in a truck?" said Ma, anxiously.
"Where's his bicycle?"

Pa waved to them gaily, ran around to the back of
the truck, and lifted out his bicycle, with the help of a
man inside. Then he waved to the driver, and the truck
moved on. Pa leaned his bicycle against the trolley car
and joined the group in the lane. He was not at all tired.
He was jaunty. He looked like a man who has con-
quered the world.

"Well, folks," he said, breezily, "I got a ride all the
way back from town. Surprised to see me so early?"

But before anybody could answer him, Pa saw Mr.
Jefferson. He let out a shout, grabbed Mr. Jefferson's
hand and pumped it up and down.

"Hello!" he exclaimed. "When did you get here? I
was looking for you. Stopped at your house. Called up

the milk company. Couldn't find you. And here you are, standing out in the road waiting for me."

"We passed each other on the road," said Mr. Jefferson. "I've been here all day, waiting for you to come back."

"Well, come on up on the porch, don't stand here," said Pa. And he led the way up the steps and leaned against the rail.

But now Ma could wait no longer to hear Pa's good news. For it must be good news. He couldn't look so gay and not have good news.

"Well, Pa?" she said.

Mr. Parker took a deep breath and looked around at the assembled company. "I got the job," he said.

"What job?" Sally asked.

"Why, the job I went for. Driving a bus."

Ma looked as if she didn't know whether to be glad or sorry. "Well, when do we start?" she asked. "My goodness, it's hard to get anything out of you, Pa."

"Start day after tomorrow," said Pa. "They were glad to see me."

"Of course. Why wouldn't they be? Well, when do we go?"

"We don't go," said Pa. "We stay here."

Mrs. Parker was exasperated. She put her hands on her hips and tossed her head. Then she said, "Now, Pa, see here. A joke is a joke, and all very well in its place. But this is too serious a matter for joking. For years

"I got the job," Pa said.

you've been saying you wouldn't drive a bus, and now you've got a job driving a bus. First you say we'll have to move, and now you say we stay here. Will you please let us know, first, what you're going to do, and secondly, what we are to do, and when we know, we'll all get busy and do it."

Then Ma sat down.

"I know, Mary," said Pa, "it's mean to tease you. But I just couldn't resist it. You see, the bus company is planning to have a new bus line between East Sawyerville and Taylorville. There's only going to be one bus in the beginning, till they see how much traffic there is. So I explained to them that as the bus would go right past our door, the natural thing would be for me to drive it. So they said it would be all right, and we can live right here, and the kids can go to school in Taylorville, for I'll take them there every morning."

"How will you take us, Pa?" Sally asked.

"Well, I'll have to get a horse, or an old car, or something. The bus garage is going to be in Taylorville, and I have to have some way of getting there, but that shouldn't be hard. And now we've got to think about fixing this place up for winter. We need a stove, and storm windows, and—well, there's a lot to do."

Pa hadn't looked tired, but now, worn out with excitement, and relief, and happiness, he sank into a chair and wiped his forehead with his handkerchief.

"Got anything to eat around here?" he asked, looking around.

"Of course," said Ma. "My goodness, the man must be starved. Here he's been providing for us, and getting a job, and we have a home and a farm and everything, and I don't even give him a bite to eat." And she began to bustle. "It's time for supper anyway," she said. "Run, Sally, run to the spring and get the butter and milk and cheese."

"We'll get an icebox," said Pa, "and I'll fix up a real kitchen here. This is all right for summer. But we're going to have a real kitchen. But say—" he looked at

Mr. Jefferson. "What about you? What are you going to do?"

They all watched and prepared to enjoy Pa's surprise when he learned of Mr. Jefferson's plans. Pa was surprised and pleased enough to satisfy anybody. He wanted to go right over to Aunt Hannah's place and see what needed to be done by way of fixing up the barn. Ma was able to persuade them all, however, to have an early supper and go over afterward, in time to help with the milking.

That evening, after the milking was done, the grown-ups sat around Aunt Hannah's kitchen table making lists. Pa and Mr. Jefferson had to go to town the next day to order supplies. They had to hurry, for Pa's job was to start in a couple of days. The regular bus trip wouldn't start till the following week, but Pa had to have a few days to get in practice first.

The children, sitting together on the porch steps, listened to the grown-up voices in the kitchen.

Ma was asking whether they really would be able to live in the trolley car when the weather got cold.

Mr. Jefferson thought that if they put enough insulation in the walls and ceiling, it would be all right. Pa said something about building a couple of rooms onto the car, and getting a good big stove to heat it.

And Aunt Hannah said, "Well, any time it gets too cold you can all come over here. We have more room here than we know what to do with."

The children looked at each other and grinned.

"Oh, boy, are we going to have fun!" said Bill. "I'm going to be a farmer, all right, and live in the country all my life."

Martha squeezed Sally's hand and said, "Any time it gets too cold in that trolley car, you come over here and sleep with me. And you can make believe you're my sister."

Suddenly Sally pointed to a star. "Look," she said. "We ought to make a wish. But I guess we don't have to. There's nothing left to wish for."

"It all came true," said George. "I wonder if it was the star that did it."

"I guess so," said Bill.

"I kind of think it was the green apple," said George. "Seems as if you ought to get a reward for doing anything as unpleasant as that."

But when they were saying goodnight, Martha whispered to Sally, "I made a wish on that star tonight."

"What did you wish?" Sally asked.

"I wished that Daddy would come home soon for a visit," said Martha.

23. SOME MORE SHOPPING

T HE NEXT DAY, old Whitey was hitched up, and
Pa, Mr. Jefferson, and all the children except Peter
climbed into the wagon. They were all going to
town. It was a celebration.

Ma and Aunt Hannah and Peter came out to wave
good-by to them.

"Now mind," said Ma. "This time don't bring back
any livestock. We have all we need."

"All right, Mary, I promise we won't," Pa called back.

It was a gay ride. All of them were in high spirits.
They made so much noise, singing and laughing and
shouting, that Whitey kept looking back with a worried
air to see what was following him.

When they had finished their shopping, and were all
sitting at the high counter in the ice cream parlor sip-
ping sodas, Mr. Jefferson whispered to Sally, "Seems to
me you're a good shopper, Sally. Come outside. I want
you to help me with some shopping."

Sally looked at him in surprise. "We'll be back soon,"

Mr. Jefferson called to the others. He led Sally along the street.

"Where are we going?" she asked.

Suddenly Mr. Jefferson turned a funny sort of red. Even his ears got red. He looked embarrassed. Then he said, "Well, you see, I didn't want to tell all the others. Martha and Tom have been told already. I told them it was a secret so they haven't said a word and nobody else knows. I thought I'd tell you, and then you could tell the others for me."

"Tell what?" Sally asked, hurrying to keep up with him and almost popping with curiosity.

Mr. Jefferson drew up to a halt in front of a jewelry store. "Come on in," he said. "This is where we go."

"I want to look at some rings," he told the clerk. "You see," he said to Sally, "it's like this. I was telling Miss Hannah, and she agreed with me, that since we were going into partnership, we might as well hitch up our horses to the same milk wagon—I mean, well, you see what I mean? No, not that kind," he said to the clerk, "nice ones. For a lady. Like that in the window." And he pointed to some very elegant and expensive-looking rings.

"Why, Mr. Jefferson!" Sally gasped. "Those are engagement rings!"

"Why, sure they are," said Mr. Jefferson, grinning from ear to ear.

"You mean—you mean," Sally stammered, "you and Aunt Hannah are going to—to get married?"

"You're a smart girl," said Mr. Jefferson. "I thought you'd catch on after a while. Now how do you like this one?" And he picked up a ring with a big sparkling stone.

"It's beautiful," Sally whispered. She felt so surprised and pleased and flattered at being asked for advice that she was a little dizzy. "It's wonderful. Can I really be the first to tell? Doesn't Ma know?"

"Nope," said Mr. Jefferson. "Not a soul except you and me and Miss Hannah and Tom and Martha. I'll take this," he said, handing the ring to the clerk, and digging in his pocket for some money. The clerk took the money respectfully, and fitted the ring into a little white velvet box.

Sally drew a deep breath, as they walked out of the store. Life seemed just one delightful surprise after another. She wondered where it would end. This couldn't go on forever. She decided to break the news at supper that evening, so she could see them all being surprised at once.

Ma and Aunt Hannah and Peter were out in front of the trolley car watching for Whitey and the milk wagon to come home.

"There they are," said Ma, as the milk wagon came into sight. "But what's that?"

Something came up behind the wagon and passed it. Something that clattered and squeaked. It made other noises too. It was full of children who shouted and laughed. It was an old green automobile. With a horrible grinding of brakes it slowed up and stopped. There was Pa at the wheel, grinning happily.

"Hello, Ma!" shouted Bill and George.

"Merciful heavens!" Ma exclaimed. "Where in the name of all that's good and beautiful did you get that? I thought I told you—"

"It's not livestock, Ma," Bill shouted. "It's just an old jalopy Pa picked up. Isn't it swell?"

"Come on, get in, we'll take you for a ride," said Pa.

"All right," said Ma. "I give up. Come, Hannah, let's take a ride."

But Aunt Hannah shook her head. "If you don't mind," she said, primly, "I prefer the milk wagon."

24. PLENTY TO BE THANKFUL FOR

EVERY MORNING, Pa would get into his jalopy and drive off to Taylorville, to get his bus. About three quarters of an hour later, the door of the trolley car would open and all the Parkers would come bouncing out. Then along would come a bus.

"Toot, toot," the horn would go. There would be Pa at the wheel. He would wave to the family and they would all wave back and shout, "Bye, Pa!" Then the bus would go off, and the Parkers would go back to their chores.

The cow had to be milked. And Kinky the kitten had learned to be on hand at milking time. Bill would shoot a stream of milk at her and she would catch it in her little pink mouth.

The chickens had to be fed. Mrs. Cluck had a fine family of chicks now, which followed her about, eating the worms she dug up for them.

The rabbits had a family too, four little brown balls of fur with big baby eyes and little white tails.

There were beans and tomatoes in the garden, and the corn was beginning to show tassels.

Ma was busy canning tomatoes, and making grape jam, and apple butter and jelly from the trees on the hill.

George's pumpkin patch was doing very well. He had a lot of small pumpkins, and Tom had showed him how to pick all the pumpkins but one off of one of the vines, so that that one would grow very large. It was enormous already, and it was still growing. Bill thought George ought to take it to the county fair, but George said he was going to give it to Mr. Jefferson and Aunt Hannah for a wedding present.

Mr. Jefferson was a dairy farmer, and a prouder dairy farmer would be hard to find. He wore overalls and a big straw hat, and the way he looked at the cows, Ma said, you'd think they were his own children.

As for Aunt Hannah, she wore a shiny ring on her finger, which she would not take off even to wash dishes. She said the luckiest day in her life was the one when she woke up and looked out of the window and saw a yellow trolley car sitting across the road.

Tom and Martha went around smiling too. For as soon as the new dairy business began to bring in profits, Tom was going to have a violin and take music lessons. And Martha had gotten over her shyness, to some extent, and was even able to sit on Mr. Jefferson's knee once in a while.

And besides, their father was coming home for

Thanksgiving. Of course Thanksgiving was a long way off, for this was only September. But school would start soon, and that would keep them busy, so that the time wouldn't seem too long. And Thanksgiving would be a good one this year, for with George's pumpkin patch, they would have enough pie to satisfy even Tom, who almost never got enough pumpkin pie.

"We certainly will have plenty to be thankful for this year," said Ma. "And it all comes of having such good neighbors."

"And children," said Pa. "Don't forget that. If you ask me, it all comes of having the children at the family conference and paying attention to what they have to say."

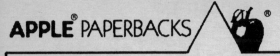

THE BABY·SITTERS CLUB®

by Ann M. Martin

Collect Them All!

The seven girls at Stoneybrook Middle School get into all kinds of adventures...with school, boys, and, of course, baby-sitting!